Plantation Tales

Other Books by Nancy Rhyne

Alice Flagg: The Ghost of the Hermitage

Carolina Seashells

Chronicles of the South Carolina Sea Islands

Coastal Ghosts

The Jack-O'-Lantern Ghost

John Henry Rutledge: The Ghost of Hampton Plantation

More Tales of the South Carolina Low Country

Murder in the Carolinas

Once Upon a Time on a Plantation

Slave Ghost Stories

The South Carolina Lizard Man

Southern Recipes and Legends

Tales of the South Carolina Low Country

Touring Coastal Georgia Backroads

Touring Coastal South Carolina Backroads

Voices of Carolina Slave Children

Plantation Tales

by Nancy Rhyne

Sandlapper Publishing Co., Inc.
Orangeburg, South Carolina

Plantation Tales

Sixth Printing, 2004

Published by Sandlapper Publishing Co., Inc.
Orangeburg, South Carolina

Manufactured in the United States of America

Rhyne, Nancy, 1926–
Plantation tales / by Nancy Rhyne.
p. cm.
Bibliography: p.
ISBN 0-87844-088-7 (hardcover); ISBN 0-87844-093-3 (paperback)
1. Tales—Southern States. 2. Plantation life—Southern States.
3. Southern States—Social life and customs. I. Title
GR108.R49 1989
398.2'7'0975—dc19 88-37029
CIP

Dedication

In loving memory, I dedicate this book to my great-grandfather, Captain James Alexander Thomas. He was born in South Carolina on August 13, 1827.

At the age of eighteen, he enlisted in a regiment that fought in the war with Mexico. Captain Thomas fought in every battle in which the militia was engaged, from the siege and capture of Vera Cruz to the capture of Mexico City, a battle in which he lost an arm. After that war, Captain Thomas entered the Citadel Academy, in Charleston.

After South Carolina seceded, preparations began for the Civil War. The state was divided into ten districts; each district was to furnish a regiment formed from the first ten companies offering their services. Captain Thomas organized and was captain of the Twenty-fourth Regiment. Many of the companies were trained by men who had received training at The Citadel.

When the war was over, my great-grandfather became a progressive farmer and the owner of several plantations as well as other landholdings. His funeral at Harmony Baptist Church in Chester County in 1906 was attended by one of the largest gatherings of people ever assembled in his part of the state.

Beside the ungathered rice he lay,
His sickle in his hand:
His breast was bare, his matted hair
Was buried in the sand.
Again, in the mist and shadow of sleep,
He saw his Native Land.

The Slave's Dream
Henry Wadsworth Longfellow

Acknowledgments

In the preparation of this manuscript, I have become firmly obliged to give thanks and credit to a lot of people. It would be almost impossible to name all of those who have assisted me . . . by inviting me into their offices and, in some instances, their plantation manor houses . . . and by telling me stories and allowing my husband to take photographs. To each of these individuals, I am grateful.

I am especially appreciative to Beverly Tetterton of the New Hanover County Library; Kenneth M. Sprunt of Orton Plantation; the staff of Chapin Memorial Library; the late Edwin O. Fulton of Wachesaw Plantation; Lucille Vanderbilt Pate, George Young, and T. N. Cox of Arcadia Plantation; Ella Severin of Hobcaw Barony; Helen Maynard of Hopsewee Plantation; Gurdon L. Tarbox Jr. and Robin Salmon of Brookgreen Gardens; the late Irvine H. Rutledge, Robert Mitchell, Will Alston, and the late Sue Alston of Hampton Plantation; Father Christian of Mepkin Abbey; Harold Lincoln of Cain Hoy Plantation; Mr. and Mrs. Robert Marvin of Walterboro; Dr. McLeod Frampton of Summerville; Mrs. Adolphus Boodle of Walterboro; Mr. Brown, superintendent of Laurel Spring Plantation; Kent Young, superintendent of Buckfield Plantation; and the staff of the chambers of commerce and historical foundations of Beaufort and Savannah.

To Amanda Gallman, of Sandlapper Publishing, I give hearty thanks for affording me the opportunity to bring full circle the plantations story.

To Barbara Stone, my editor, thank you for your wisdom, your friendship, and your good-hearted nature. You have made this book a more important experience. I'm happy you're my friend.

And, as always, hurray for Sid! Once again he helped me every step of the way in getting the book together. His photographs add so much to my stories. It isn't always the easiest thing in the world to get clear photographs, especially when the weather doesn't cooperate. Somehow, though, he manages to pull it off.

Nancy Rhyne
Myrtle Beach, South Carolina

Introduction

Some people have had a glimpse of the Low Country's plantation past—a look at her vast and imposing landscapes, a taste of her sensuality and complexity. Although the age of peacocks, palaces, and Charleston balls is long over, magnificent mansions and descendants of the planter families remain. The allure and charm of that time lingers, especially along the strip of Low Country between Wilmington, North Carolina, and Savannah, Georgia.

Searching for stories for my books takes me to many places. I once found myself sitting in the elegant plantation drawing room of a Vanderbilt. Other times, I have visited cabins practically hidden from civilization, where I had to park my car beside the road and walk over dirt paths into the woods or to a river. On one occasion, I made my way to an old sawmill. Several times throughout my journeying I had to stop the car in the middle of the road to allow a canebrake rattler to continue on its way. On one trip, I made eye contact with a deer whose expression let me know that I was intruding on his territory.

I would not trade a minute of the past twenty-something years. My husband Sid and I have clocked hundreds of hours on southern back roads. But we've always been successful. The people were friendly and eager to talk, and they shared with me the stories for which I'd searched—and much more.

This edition includes nine new tales. These introduce the reader to wealthy *Yankees* who decided to buy for themselves pieces of our southern paradise. Around the turn of the twentieth century nearly all of the Old South plantations were on the market. Heirs could no longer make millions growing the crops of their forefathers. And they were unable to cover the cost of taxes or the enormous upkeep.

As the plantations were perfect for hunting preserves, prominent northerners began locating the many-acred estates and plunked down cash on the spot to acquire them.

But, isolation in splendor does have its price. The old plantations, which often extended from a river to the ocean, were not for those who were timid. Nevermind the initial cost of the property, but the land had often been in the possession of families who had lived on the property for generations. And the people were as much a part of the treasured landscape as the oak-lined avenues and the mansions with their fourteen-foot ceilings and stately white pillars. To top it off, the old houses sometimes came with ghosts or stories of evil spirits or creatures that walked in the night, like boo-daddies and plat-eyes.

In the 1920s, 30s, and 40s, signatures such as Huntington, Baruch, duPont, Hutton, Field, Vanderbilt, Luce, Roosevelt, Doubleday, and Marshall began to appear on deeds. Inspired by the perfection of the landscape, the new owners chose to maintain the dignity of the land—leaving legacies of ancient trees, pristine water, magnificent homes, and native wildlife undisturbed. The properties stand today much as they did in earlier times.

"Nowhere else in the world," wrote Archibald Rutledge, South Carolina poet laureate and heir to Hampton Plantation, "has nature been kinder to her children than in those regions where the great plantations were formed out of the Eden-like wilderness of the Low Country. And that charm is an eternal one; though the civilization that it cradled and nourished has passed away, the charm survives."

Nancy Rhyne
January 1999

Contents

The Millionaire Planters and The Gifted Slaves

(A Prologue)

At the risk of sacrilege, it is possible to imagine that writers of fictional Southern romance invented the Old South. Or at least they improvised, it seems, on pillared mansions behind moss-draped oaks. And, for that matter, they fabricated Southern belles in billowy hoop skirts. For more than forty years, writers have created and recreated a make-believe Old South of splendor and beauty. But their stories don't come close to equalling the plantations and style of life from Wilmington to Savannah during the days of rice culture.

Among America's most prestigious addresses from the mid-1700s to 1860 were the plantations adjacent to the rivers that emptied into the Atlantic from Wilmington, North Carolina to Savannah, Georgia. These plantations were the scene of an Old Guard life-style that was more exciting than any fictional description ever written and surely Hollywood has never created anything that came even close. The planters were the richest people in the land, except for families like the Astors and Rockefellers. The immense family fortunes that were accumulated along those coastal rivers supplied the means with which to create a culture unusual in colonial America.

The planter families vacationed abroad. Their children were taught by tutors imported from England, France and Germany, while governesses came from New England or Europe. They built fine manor houses, usually black cypress (heart cypress) and heart yellow pine. Their furniture came from England or was made in the popular European styles by artisans on the plantations. Their dining room sideboards held shining silver, along with fine china and crystal from England.

Rice brought sky-high prices in England, and cotton never brought the income that rice did. Consequently, the mansions in *Gone With The Wind* look like Chicken Coop Village when compared with the manor houses of these rice planters. They were wealthy and they flaunted their wealth, especially in their homes, which were judged as an indication of prosperity. The mansion was the pulse-point of the huge estate.

One planter who became governor of South Carolina desired a collection of art second to no other in the parish. He commissioned the famous Charleston portraitist Thomas Sully to attend a sale of paintings in Baltimore. There was obviously no limit to the budget. Sully returned to the plantation with: *A Turk's Head,* by Rembrandt; *The Supper at Emmaus,* by Gherardo del Notte; *The Holy Family,* a tapestry for which Sully was offered twice the price he had paid; *Io,* a large and beautiful canvas which shows a heifer chewing her cud as she is watched by Cerberus, while on the other side of a mountain Mercury plays his flute; *Saint Paul on the Island of Melita,* a large canvas which depicts Saint Paul dramatically shaking his finger at a viper; and *Saint Peter in Prison,* which shows Saint Peter being awakened by an angel as his captors sleep.

Reflecting on Sully's choices, the planter/buyer, Robert Francis Withers Allston, said he believed the collection would create in his children an appreciation for and recognition of fine paintings.

Plantation verandas faced the rivers in order to get the breeze, and it was here that family members often read. Each house had an exceptional library which contained practically all the French classics, especially those of the eighteenth century, including the works of Voltaire, Racine, Corneille, Montesquieu and others. There were first editions of nearly everything worthwhile in English, from Milton all the way to sets of sermons and prayers.

Parties in the mansion ballrooms were original and soul-stirring. Each plantation had its own little slave ensemble which provided music. At Brookgreen Plantation, near Murrells Inlet, South Carolina, the band consisted of three brothers: Divine, Daniel, and Summer Horry.

Besides their wonderful manor houses, the planters owned townhouses in Wilmington, Charleston, or Savannah. The Burgwin-Wright House, at Third and Market streets in Wilmington, is an excellent example of a town residence. With the marriage of Margaret Haynes to John Burgwin, two enormous plantation incomes were combined. Burgwin built this magnificent townhouse in which the interior woods were brought directly from England in 1770. The house is open to the public today.

In Charleston, the planters' townhouses carried elegance to new heights. There were exquisitely carved mouldings, some made in England and others crafted by local artisans. Mirrors from Europe hung on the walls, and there were so many portraits of family members on display that local, as well as, itinerant artists must have been kept busy.

The social season in Charleston began in February and lasted until Lent. During that time Charleston's planter families were kept busy with balls and horse racing. The St. Cecilia Society sponsored a ball every ten days, and these balls were the most original and exciting of all. But the Jockey Club ball, which was held at the end of a week of horse racing, was the largest.

When attending the races, the men left their Charleston houses early, and the ladies rode over later "in full feather," according to J. Motte Alston. A grandson of William Alston, who had a passion for racing fine horses, Motte Alston says that a coach bearing the family coat of arms and pulled by four matching bay horses carried his grandmother to the racetrack. Like all other wives of planters, she was adorned in clothes and jewels from Paris.

Charleston parents kept tabs on their youngsters, but it wasn't so difficult because everyone made appointments to meet days in advance. When one young girl answered the request for a social call, she was scolded by her mother for having answered the note in the first person. "You should have said that Miss Allston regrets that she will not be able to ride with Mr. Ravenel."

Adele Allston of Chicora Wood Plantation was married in the Nathaniel Russell House at 51 Meeting Street. (This house is open to the public.) The wedding ceremony was held in the ballroom, an elegant room with a high ceiling, and the four ceiling-to-floor windows on the south opened onto a balcony. White panes of glass on the other windows in the room were fitted with mirrors to give the illusion of a crowded room. The rosewood furniture was upholstered in blue velvet with pink rosebuds, and the carpet was like velvet, with bouquets of pink roses for decoration. The white mantel was carved with dancing women holding aloft garlands of flowers.

Like Charleston, Savannah's aura was opulence, and the golden living was truly unalloyed in this important seaport which sent the products of the planters to England. Although rice was planted into the 20th century by the rivers to the north, rice culture was all but eliminated by the scourge of yellow fever which swept Savannah in 1820. Now Savannah's "good old days" are back. The 1977 multi-million dollar riverfront revitalization peaked the restoration effort in Savannah's Historic District, and many beautiful townhouses of the planters are open to the public.

The rice planters moved around from season to season for reasons of amusement and health. August and September were called "the sickly months" because of the danger of contracting malaria from the bites of the anopheles mosquito. Planters and physicians alike believed the malady to be caused by the stagnant swamps and the damp Spanish moss that hung from live oaks. So many people died from malaria during the summer months that when the planters and their families returned to town "after the first frost," their first question was, "Who died while we were away?" The slaves who attended to the planting and cultivating of rice during the summer months were immune to malaria because of their hereditary sickle cell which although it gave them immunity to malaria has been cited as the source of sickle cell anemia.

In order to avoid the dreaded malarial fever, the planters moved their families to the seashore portion of their plantations or to beach houses they had built on the shore or barrier islands. Many of the planters in the Waccamaw region of South Carolina built cottages at Pawley's Island, and some of those houses remain today. The visitor gets a good glimpse of the old houses while traveling Pawley's one road which runs between the houses and "the creek" (the marsh). Piers jut into the marsh where crabs are netted; blue crabs are a staple in Pawley's Island diets even today. The ocean is on the other side of the old houses.

God made the earth, and the planters made Pawley's Island, some say. But God had a lot to do with this place, too, for it is here that shore birds flock, breezes never stop blowing, and no commercial structure or enterprise is permitted. Visitors either love this quiet offshore place, or the old ramshackle houses don't appeal to them at all.

The daughter of one planter wrote in her journal of the toilsome and strenuous move from the plantation to Pawley's Island. Her father's entire household migrated from the plantation, which was four miles from the island "as the crow flies." They traveled seven miles in a rowboat and four miles by land, however, in order to reach Pawley's. Horses, cows, furniture, bedding, trunks and provisions were all put onto large flat raft-like boats, some sixty by twenty feet and others ever larger, at dawn, and sent ahead. Then the family was rowed down the river. The oarsmen sang spirituals as they rowed, keeping time with the pulling of the oars. Occasionally their songs would be interrupted by a shout of "Alligator!" There were six oarsmen in that planter family's boat, and they sang "In case I never see you any more, I'm hopes to meet you on Canaan's happy shore." They also sang "Roll, Jordan, Roll," and "Oh, Zion."

In her journal the daughter also described life at Pawley's in those days:

> We went to our summer home on Pawleys Island in June, and oh! the delight of the freedom of the life on the sea-beach. The glorious surf bathing early in the morning. We often saw the sun rise while we were in the water, for we were a very early household, and had breakfast at an unearthly hour.
> . . . We were required to read and write and practice every day. Papa's rules were strict: We could never go out to walk or play on the beach in the afternoon unless we had done our tasks. I was required to practice (piano) only half an hour, but it must be done. Then I wrote a page in a blank book and showed it to Mamma for correction. She had me to write a journal of all that had taken place the day before. . . . Then I read to Mamma from some classic for half an hour, so I did not go wild during the holidays. Add to this that Papa did not allow us to read a story-book or a novel before the three-o'clock dinner, so that I read by myself in the mornings Motley's *Rise of the Dutch Republic* and Prescott's *Phillip II*, only a little portion every day, but there is no telling how much my taste was formed by it.

Although fish were netted each day for the tables in the planters' beach cottages, vegetables were brought regularly from the plantations. Almost everything that one needed for a nutritious diet was provided from the plantations. Vegetables came from the gardens, sugar cane was raised for a sweetener, and salt was obtained by evaporating sea water. In 1850 from the gardens at Brookgreen Plantation came 66,000 bushels of sweet potatoes, and there were always thousands of bushels of rice. Point Peter, a plantation located on the northeast and northwest branches of the Cape Fear River, near Wilmington produced 75 bushels of rice per acre. The plantation consisted of 3,000 acres.

To live in the manner of the rice planters required an enormous labor force. Each planter owned many slaves; some owned hundreds. Slaves attended to the planter families' every need. Besides coopers, tanners, carpenters and field workers, there were dog-minders, cat-minders and a fly-brush boy who waved the turkey tail fan over the table to shoosh away flies. One servant in a plantation manor house was assigned the task of opening and closing windows. And dozens of other tasks were performed.

The slaves were stable, skillful, and competent. They were also enormously gifted in imagery and harmony. But just like anyone who has been yanked from one environment and thrust into another, their old customs, beliefs and practices were difficult to abolish. As an example, they preferred "irregular" healers to qualified physicians. One such healer in the Waccamaw region was Aunt Liza, who made her medicines from ingredients she gathered in the woods and fields. From weeds she would blend a bitter tea that caused profuse perspiration and proved effective in curing fever. She made a tonic by gathering cinders from a blacksmith's shop, pounding them into a fine powder, and adding molasses and ginger to make the mixture taste good. Aunt Liza also cultivated certain plants for their roots, which she tied in little bags. Black snakeroot and Sampson snakeroot were two ingredients that went into the bags, which were sewn into the seams of her skirts. A wave or two of Aunt Liza's skirts was sometimes all it took to cure an illness.

What the slaves believed, they believed perfectly. They accepted as absolute truth the fact that certain unearthly beings lived in the woods of this area. Stories of these creatures were told over and over, even whispered into the ear of an infant being nursed by some old mammy, while the child's mother worked in the rice fields. These tales passed from generation to generation, tales of hags, hants, plat-eye, boo-daddies and ghosts.

Hags: There were two well-defined beliefs about hags. One persuasion (the predominant one) said that a hag was the disembodied spirit of an old woman who practiced witchcraft. The hag freed herself from the body of the woman after darkness set in and returned to the body at "second fowl crow." During night hours, the hag plagued the people whom the woman had been paid to harm. Sometimes a hag would slip from the skin of a living person and go about causing trouble, such as "riding" a person. There are many accounts of "a hag ride me!" status. Aunt Hagar, born during Sherman's march, said, "Hags suck you! Draw your blood! I feared of hag."

Hants: A hant could change from the body of a person to a ghost at will. Most people prevented hants from coming into their houses by placing a hair brush or flour sifter inside the front door. The theory of this preventative was that when the hant entered the door and saw the brush or sifter, it would stop to count the hairs in the brush or the holes in the sieve. By the time it had completed counting, the sun would have risen and the hant would disappear.

"There was a hant in Tom Pryor's house all right," said Martha. "Wouldn't give no rest a-tall. Terrible! Come in there and had more noise on that stove than enough. He always came in the kitchen and cut up all his craziness in there."

A plat-eye had the distinct characteristic of being able to change from one creature to another at will. Addie, of Murrells Inlet, explained.

"Plat-eye? Yes'm. The old folks talk bout plat-eye. They say they take the shape of all kind of critter—dog, cat, hog, mule, varmint—and I hear tell of plat-eye takin' form of gator.

"You know that little swampy place behind the parsonage?" Addie continued. "Well, one time I had my bloom on me. It was dark. I wasn't feared none a-tall. I brush the weepin' moss aside and I travel in my bare feet and my shoes been tied to my girdle string. And when I come to the footlog, I could see same as I see you now. I could see that same old cypress tree what's there now.

"And I see Mr. Bull Frog hit the water, ker-plunk. And a cooter slid off the log at my feet. And I 'clare to God, when I looked up that cooter been turned to a cat. A black cat with his eyes like balls of fire. And his back arched up, and his tail twissin', and switchin', and his hair standin' on end."

A tiny church with bell tower is among the slave cabins at a Low Country plantation.

Photograph by SID RHYNE.

Working in the rice fields. Note the canals used for flooding the low-lying fields.

From the W.D. Morgan and A.G. Trenholm collections at Georgetown County Memorial Library.

The late DuBose Heyward—who wrote *Porgy*, the book that was the basis for the folk opera *Porgy and Bess*—spoke of plat-eye as being a varmint that would try to lure its victims away from buried treasure. Many valuables of the manor houses, including china and silver, were buried during the Civil War years, and there was a common belief that plat-eye guarded the treasure. If anyone other than the owner of the valuables approached, the plat-eye would divert the person's attention from the spot.

George Brown saw a plat-eye in the form of a black hog with enormous white tusks. At other times it was a five-legged calf or a hunchback yellow dog with two tails.

Boo-daddies were spirits of conjur-doctors that escaped the physical bodies of the conjurers at night but kept the physical shapes of those irregular physicians. (Conjur-doctors were said to be unusual in appearance; Obie Hines was such a medical man, and he had a "funny-shaped head.") Conjur rituals involved the use of cemetery dirt and other fearful materials, and conjurers were said to be able to cast or remove jinxes and spells.

Ghosts were everywhere. One woman's description of a ghost went like this: "It wuz the terriblest lookin sight. It walked ten feet offen the ground." Ghosts were very real to the slaves, who believed they knew exactly where ghosts were to be seen, their familiar haunts, the time they left their graves and the time of their return.

These people, who believed so strongly in the creatures of another world, were just as zealous regarding their religion. Adult slaves had their own "pray houses," where they worshipped frequently when no ordained clergyman was available. Their class leader held forth, conducting highly emotional services, largely of singing, hand-clapping and quoting Biblical passages to the accompaniment of the congregation's "Amens."

The praise groups, spicy mixes of dissimilar temperaments, goals, and ages, were concocted with the effect of maximizing every conceivable feeling, and they yielded unabashed emotion. As Aunt Hagar explained, "Down, down, down. When they hold them good meeting and I ain't there, you know I down. That man preach! He preach Mother's Day till he preach me out of me sense. Had Rachel's baby in me arms. Preacher ring out on Mother's Day and I had to pitch baby up."

In 1829 the religious life of the slaves entered into a period that is remembered to this day as one of the most inspiring periods of their history. Dr. Alexander Glennie began his work at All Saints Church in the Waccamaw region and made it known that he believed the planters' lack of spiritual attention to their slaves was an abomination to the Lord. Glennie persuaded the planters to build chapels where slaves could worship on their plantations. On horseback, he made his way by gutted roadways to the plantations to give religious instruction. When this beloved man was expected, the slaves responded with near-perfect attendance at chapel.

There were several ingredients that made this coastal area ideal for the production of rice. The soil of the coast was born of detritus deposited by rivers flowing to the sea eras ago; these ancient deposits, so rich and loamy, resulted in earth that was near perfect for the growing of rice. Rivers throughout this area had a proper "pitch of the tide" that enabled the adjoining fields to be flooded and drained as tides rose and fell. An additional benefit of the rivers was their convenience for transporting supplies, produce and people. During the peak rice-growing years, they were crowded with vessels and were the major means of transportation. Each plantation had a landing and boats for various purposes.

And finally, slaves were a very important part of the formula that made the region from Wilmington to Savannah colorful as well as wealthy. A hardy slave labor force was available to clear the fields adjacent to the rivers, during the growing season and harvesting the product.

In 1665 the captain of a Madagascan ship gave Landgrave Smith, of Charleston, a peck of rice seed (paddy or rice in husk), and told him that this was good and valuable food and advised its cultivation in the colony. The result was that seed rice was distributed among certain planters, one of whom was Stephen Bull, the wealthy English founder of Sheldon, on the Broad River near Beaufort, South Carolina. Rice culture proceeded at a phenomenal rate, and the profitableness of the crop was as great as was its momentum. (From *Beaufort County, South Carolina: The Shrines, Early History and Topography,* Willet, Augusta, Georgia, 1929.) By the 1730s, the land where diamondback rattlers grew to be more than seven feet long had come under more intensive cultivation, and export figures had almost doubled. By 1740 rice exports had more than doubled again.

There are still people living who can tell what it was like when rice was sovereign. They can describe the process of cultivation from the clearing of the swamps for a rice field to the sale of the product.

According to the late Edwin O. Fulton of Wachesaw Plantation, Murrells Inlet, every available inch of land adjacent to the rivers and beyond the reach of salt water was cleared for rice fields. There was an almost solid mass of growth—cypress trees, gum trees, and vines—to be cleared before a field could be used. After the land was cleared, canals were dug to direct the tidal waters into the fields and rice-trunk-docks (doors) were constructed and placed at the mouths of the canals to regulate the flow of the tidal waters.

Each March the land was harrowed and trenches were dug twelve inches apart, leaving room for a specially designed jack hoe which would cultivate between the rows. In April seeds were planted, and after the planting of seed, the doors of the rice-trunk-docks were opened, and water coming in on the next high tide flowed into the canals and covered the fields. The sprout flow sheltered the seed for up to six days, or until it had sprouted; then the fields were drained and the sprouts were allowed to grow in the sun until they were about six inches high.

The next flooding was called the "long flow." It completely covered the young plants, floating away debris and insects. The rice plants were kept under water by this flow for more than twenty days. Following the long flow, the plants were dried out and again hoed. There was still another flooding of the fields, the lay-by-flow, before the rice harvest which began in August or September.

As the rice-growing season advanced, a change in the color of the fields took place. The fields which began as green gradually were mingled with yellow as the grain ripened. Eventually, the yellow predominated over green until the fields, as far as one could see, looked alive, shifting with the wind, sunshine and the shadows of passing clouds. Finally the mass of gold was ready for the reapers' hooks.

Women cut the rice. They cut three rows at a time, grasping the stalks with their left hands and using sickles in their right hands. They laid the stalks on the stubble in order that the sun might dry the rice. One woman's rice cutting task was a half-acre, and good workers performed their tasks in about two hours. The fol-

This woman is pounding rice with the use of a mortar and pestle.
From the W.D. Morgan and A.G. Trenholm collections at Georgetown County Memorial Library.

lowing day they tied the stalks into bundles and stacked them in the fields.

As soon as the sheaves of rice were stacked in the barnyards, the planters began to fret over possible hurricanes. Rice harvesting coincided with the time of year when storms brewed in the tropics, usually assaulting the coast from Wilmington to Savannah and occasionally destroying whole crops of rice. Such a storm, on September 27, 1822, was reported in the *Winyaw Intelligencer,* a Georgetown newspaper: "Injury sustained in crops must necessarily be great," the report read, "as much of the rice which was harvested has been flown out of the barnyards and dispersed—many Negroes have been killed and most of the barns and mills have been unroofed and [rice] trunks and banks torn to pieces."

In good years, rice was carried to mills to be cleaned, changing the product from "rough" rice to "clean" rice. Almost all rice plantations had their own rice mills capable of threshing from 600 to 1200 bushels per day. The mills usually consisted of three buildings: a conveyor house into which the bundles of rice were thrown from the wagons; the mill proper, a two-story building containing all the machinery; and a rice house where the product was stored while awaiting shipment to market. A "conveyor cloth" ran from the conveyor house to the second story of the mill, and on it the bundles of rice were carried to the "beater," where the grain was threshed from straw and chaff. Iron rakes within the beater box moved the straw to chute which carried it to wagons waiting to haul it away.

The grains of rice threshed from straw were passed through a fan on the first floor of the mill. The fan blew away the refuse, leaving rice still enclosed in its hulls. Then the product was again taken to the second story of the mill, where it was passed through a sieve which removed any chaff, sand and weed seeds that remained. The grain was then sent to shelling stones, which rolled in opposing directions with a small space between them. As the rice passed between the massive granite wheels, the hulls were cracked. The hulls were removed by using a mortar and pestle.

Rice was packed in barrels and sent to a factor for sale. As soon as a sale was completed, the factor sent his client (the planter) a statement. From the sale price, certain charges were deducted, including the factor's commission. For many years the price of rice was stable. A Charleston publication entitled *Wholesale Commodity Prices, 1790–1861* reveals that the price for rice in 1817 was seven cents per pound. It was six cents per pound in 1805, a year when one South Carolina planter noted a profit of $120,000. J. Motte Alston wrote that prior to the Civil War the price for rice in the rough ranged from $.75 to $1.00 per bushel, and for clean rice from $2.75 to $5.00 per hundred pounds, but only choice rice brought the top price. After the Civil War, the average prices of rice ranged between four and a half and five and a half cents per pound, and there were about forty-five pounds per bushel, which netted $1.10 to $1.40 f.o.b. the plantation.

One can envision the rivers during the fall of the year, crowded with boats of rice on the way to market. Some planters had their own vessels to transport their product, while others rented boats when they needed to ship their rice. In 1749 Thomas Lynch of Hopsewee Plantation, on the North Santee River, owned a twenty-ton schooner with a partner and he also owned interest in another schooner. The Horrys and Rutledges of Hampton Plantation, on the South Santee River, owned their own vessels which took their rice directly to England.

And just how did the planters come to own such enormous tracts of land? The English Lords Proprietors offered attractive terms to bring settlers to the territory in the late 17th century. Under their feudalistic plan for granting land, there were three categories of grants: seigniories which would go to the Lords Proprietors; baronies which would be granted to members of nobility, and plantations and farms which would go to commoners who could provide slaves to produce materials for export. Quit-rents were to go to the Lords Proprietors. When the king took jurisdiction over land grants in 1729, quit-rents went to the royal treasury and baronies were discontinued. Plantations continued to be granted as before.

To request a grant of land, a person went before the royal governor and council. If the request was approved, a warrant was issued to have the land surveyed. The surveyor-general returned the warrant and a certificate of survey to the register to record. After the plat was recorded, the grantee took an oath pledging allegiance, faithfulness and obedience to the crown. Heads of families usually received 150 acres, as well as smaller tracts for each member of the household. Slaves were counted as members of families for purposes of land grants.

The colonists in the coastal region came mainly from three sources: Englishmen seeking new opportunities, Scots in search of mercantile establishment, and French Huguenots looking for land and religious freedom. By 1706 the Anglican Church was established in the colony, and parishes were laid out. Each parish was supposed to build a church, provide for a clergyman and maintain a record of births, burials, marriages and christenings. The parishes were important to the province because in addition to their religious duties they undertook some of the duties of a local government, such as caring for the poor.

Most of the plantation owners were connected by blood or by marriage, which leads to the conclusion that planters were like one large family in perfect control of their destinies. John Allston was born in England in 1666 and came to this country between 1685 and 1694. He started a Low-Country dynasty that seemed to agree on everything except how to spell the family name. William

Working a rice field on the Waccamaw River by using a team of oxen.
Courtesy of Brookgreen Gardens.

Alston of Clifton Plantation, on Waccamaw River—called "King Billy" due to his wealth and prestige—dropped one of the *l*s and started a line of one-l Alstons. The Allstons and Alstons were especially interesting and extensive, with a startling display of plantations.

From the late 1700s to 1860 a golden age existed along the coast from Wilmington to Savannah. No person could have better described it than the late Archibald Rutledge, of Hampton Plantation on the South Santee River, and Poet Laureate of South Carolina. "Nowhere else in the world has nature been kinder to her children," wrote Rutledge, "than in those regions where the great plantations were formed out of the Eden-like wilderness of the Low Country. And that charm is an eternal one; though the civilization that it cradled and nourished has passed away, the charm survives. The home remains lovely after the guests are gone."

The munificent life that was lived on the rice plantations during the golden age is one of the social feats of the centuries. From the planters and slaves, from plantations and cabins, from the extraordinary lifestyle and the blooming force of nature, narratives inevitably came. While the tales that follow are steeped in folklore and emotion, they provide a look down the long corridors of a radiant, romantic time. We see a landscape that we might want to inhabit, but we are merely tourists traveling through the tales.

Author's Note

Traditionally, my tales have come from the rice-planting region which was from the Cape Fear River in North Carolina to the Savannah area. This region is the coastal land where the soil, lowlands and tidewater were more suitable for the production of this grain. Additionally, many of the slaves who worked in the rice fields were gifted storytellers, and some remained for a time after the Civil War. Work in the rice fields was less strenuous than work in the cotton fields. As a result of the perfect formula for rice production and the people who entertained themselves with the telling of stories, this region became rich in folklore. However, as readers go down the coast through my books, they sometimes ask why my collections are more fertile in stories from the Waccamaw River to Charleston section than from the Wilmington and Savannah areas. There *is* a reason.

From Orton Plantation up the Cape Fear River, rice plantations thrived. North of Lilliput was the plantation of T. Cowan. This plantation had 160 acres of rice land. Continuing upriver Clarendon came next. Two hundred and twenty-five acres were planted in rice, averaging seventy-two bushels per acre. To mention others, there were Mallory, Gravely, Belvidere, The Forks, Buchioi, and many more.

Few of these plantations remain today, and yet many people are unable to grasp this fact. Most of the manor houses were of frame construction, and with the invasion of hurricanes and hostile armies, they have not survived.

The same is true of Savannah. Take The Hermitage: In June 1935 the Savannah Port Authority gave the Union Bag and Paper Corporation of the state of New Jersey a ninety-nine year lease on The Hermitage with an option to purchase. In a short time a huge paper mill was erected near the mansion, utilizing the old buildings as part of the Diamond Match Company.

As for Royal Vale Plantation, by the river where plantation buildings once stood are now factories, warehouses, naval stores yards, and railroad spurs. And famous Mulberry Grove today is a deserted wilderness. Marsh grass has taken over where rice plants once waved in the breeze, and dry canals are covered with vines and bushes.

For some reason the plantations of the Waccamaw River to Charleston region have, at least in part, survived. And there were people who took the time to record dozens of stories about these plantations and the people who lived there. That is why the tales of this section are more abundant.

While I have spent many years in research, have visited the sites and have endeavored to write these stories with historical content as well as entertainment values there were occasional gaps in some of the tales. In order to close the interspace, I wrote those stories in the manner my research indicates would have been as near the original as possible.

Plantation Tales

A copy of one of Minnie Evans' paintings on display at the St. John's Museum of Art, Inc., 114 Orange Street, Wilmington, N.C.
Photograph by ST. JOHN'S MUSEUM OF ART, INC.

"Someone Had My Hand"

The face in the painting looks straight at you. On the sides of the head, where the ears should be, are profiles of the countenance, showing a strong forehead, delicate nose, lips and chin. There are other subjects in the same painting, including a unicorn. The animal has not only the single straight horn with a spiral twist, but wings. It is said that unicorns have to be more than 200 years old to have wings. The artist's name, scribbled in third-grade style, is in a lower corner of the painting, which hangs on a wall on the third floor of the St. Johns Art Gallery, on Orange Street in Wilmington, North Carolina.

Most viewers wonder for a moment if the painting is a gap in their artistic education. Then they shrug and move on. A story goes with the painting—and the artist Minnie Evans.

Minnie Jones was born on December 12, 1892 in the Long Creek community of Pender County. Having grown up in Wilmington, in 1903 she moved to the Wrightsville Sound area where she worked as a "sounder," selling oysters and clams door to door. In 1908 Minnie married Julius Evans, a servant to Pembroke Jones.

Seven miles east of Wilmington and two miles southeast of US 17 at Oleander Drive and Airlie Road lies Airlie Gardens, originally a 150-acre estate settled by Pembroke Jones.

An executive of the Atlantic Coast Line Railroad, Jones named his plantation after his Scottish ancestors. Airlie Plantation was very exotic by the standards of its day. Jones built a hunting lodge with Italian stone fireplaces, and the building was designed by John Russell Pope, the designer of the Jefferson Memorial and the National Gallery of Art in Washington, D. C. Governors, senators, ambassadors, and business and social friends, including

Vanderbilts and Harrimans, visited Jones at the lodge.

Pembroke Jones also constructed a mansion of more than thirty rooms, including a ballroom and banquet room large enough for entertaining eighty people. The mansion also included eleven baths, about twenty dressing rooms, and elaborate parlors and recreation facilities. The garden was kept in perfect order by Topel, a German gardener who at one time had served Kaiser Wilhelm. The azalea and camellia gardens were personally developed under the supervision of Mrs. Jones.

On Good Friday in 1935, something happened to Minnie Evans, the wife of a servant in the Pembroke Jones' mansion. While Minnie was sleeping, the Lord visited her. He said, "Minnie, I am your Lord, Jehovah. I am going to take care of you and you are going to paint." As the Lord spoke, Minnie saw sky, trees, flowers, faces, animals and a whole new world, all in pictures.

"A beautiful light appeared in my room" Minnie said later. She went on to explain that there was a large wreath. She didn't actually see the wreath, but she saw the shadow of the wreath, and from behind the shadow came the light.

"I became very happy, and I had to get out of bed and praise God for that," Minnie said. "And God talked to me. He said, 'This light that you see shall shine around you. I am Jehovah, your God.' "

The next day Minnie drew a picture of what she had seen in her vision the night before. The following night she had another vision, and another the night after that. Finally, the Jones family provided her with canvas and water colors to use in recreating her mistifying visions.

In 1948 Airlie Plantation, then described as being about 160 acres, was sold for approximately $150,000 to W. A. Corbett and his wife. The new owner was approached about opening Airlie for tourists expected to be drawn to Wilmington for its first Azalea Festival. Corbett was owner and operator of Corbett Package Company, and had also built a vast business out of North Carolina sweet potatoes.

Airlie's terrain was a mixture of styles of beauty. Near the mansion were thousands of camellias, azaleas, roses, and numerous other species of shrubs and flowers. White and black swan swam on ponds and lakes. Spacious driveways cut through forests of huge trees and other lush growth. The mansion was in fairly good condition; however, vandals had taken their toll on the

Pembroke Jones hunting lodge.

Airlie Plantation was opened to the public, and renamed Airlie Gardens. The owners hired Minnie Evans as a gatekeeper. It was believed that Minnie would be the perfect person to welcome visitors. As a granddaughter of slaves, she was full of stories. Her forebears had come from Trinidad, in the Caribbean Sea, but they had left Trinidad seven generations earlier. Besides her gift as a storyteller, Minnie's paintings were unusual, to say the least.

Day after day, Minnie Evans sat at the Airlie hand-forged gate, hammered in the shapes of leaves and flowers. She collected $1 entrance fees from those who came to enter the gate and travel a winding road bordered by magnolia, rare camellias, and moss-draped oaks that were among the finest specimens in the South. "Miz Minnie," as she was affectionately called, was as popular with Wilmington residents as with visitors from faraway places.

Minnie's mother lived with Minnie and her husband. Minnie said that she was having so many visions by this time, and painting so many pictures, that her mother thought she was crazy.

"Late one evening when the moon was at its height," Minnie said, "my friends and I were outside looking at it. Around the moon I saw a circle and in the circle were faces of animals. There were rainbows, and at the end of them were two lions. I asked my pastor what was the meaning of the lions. He told me that those were the lions of Judea. So I painted my vision just as I remembered it, with the two lions."

Minnie Evans had numerous dreams about angels. She called them "imitations of angels." She said that she did not believe there was an artist who could paint an angel because angels come from the throne of God. "We can get the imitation, but we can't paint the *real* angel."

Minnie's paintings were done in the mixed media of ink, crayon, water color, oils, and she also created collages from parts of her drawings. Her work went unnoticed until 1959 when a New York photographer, traveling through Wilmington, saw them. This resulted in a New York exhibition, and Minnie Evans was no longer Wilmington's well-kept secret.

Her works were shown for the first time in New York City in 1966 at the Church of Epiphany. Another show followed at The Art Image Gallery on 64th Street. The dark-skinned lady who had been born in a log cabin smiled as she heard for the first

Minnie Evans.
Photograph by DAN SEARS, Wilmington Star-News.

time that an article written about her work appeared in the August 4, 1969 edition of *Newsweek.*

By that time, Minnie was a widow. She was living surrounded by four generations of family—her 90-year-old mother, three children, various grandchildren and great-grandchildren. When asked about her paintings, she still said, "They's a puzzlement to me!"

"Mama has six pictures in the White House," her son George said. "They are there now. In the art gallery. Russia has six of them, and Queen Elizabeth has twelve. Every couple of months Queen Elizabeth would write her a letter. I have a bunch of that stuff. China has six of her pictures. She had letters from people all the time, asking for her pictures. Every month she had a letter from Washington.

"She had many visions. One almost every night. In the morning, she'd say, 'I had another dream last night. I saw what I was to paint. I got out of bed and painted, but I'll finish it up today.' "

Despite her phenomenal success, Minnie had to wrestle with her family and with her conscience to win acceptance for the idea that a woman of her background could be an artist. Coming to terms with her place in the world of artists was a difficult process. Born into a society where workaday values were more appropriate, Minnie shaped her character and gave form to her artistic talent by continuing to be a gatekeeper until her health failed.

"She hasn't painted any since about the late nineteen seventies," her son said. "She was in bad health when she had to give up her job at the gate at Airlie, and I'm glad. The next gatekeeper was robbed. The Good Lord just took her away in the nick of time. I'm glad He did."

Some other relics of romantic Airlie were gone by the time Minnie resigned her job. The mansion had been destroyed by fire, and the hunting lodge had been ruined by vandalism long before that.

Minnie had scant definition for her imagery and symbols. "My whole life has been dreams and visions," she said. "Someone had my hand." However, this unusual artist had received international recognition for her paintings which were displayed in New York, London, Saranac Lake, Raleigh and Wilmington.

Minnie Evans spent her last years in a nursing home in Wilmington where she died. To the very end she said that Someone had her hand.

Orton Plantation manor house.
Photograph by SID RHYNE.

Dr. James Sprunt encouraged his wife, the former Luola Murchison, to add the wings to Orton house, and to design and plant the gardens. At her death in 1916 Dr. Sprunt had the Orton chapel built as a memorial to her. It is called Luola's Chapel, and it's located in a spectacularly beautiful part of the garden at Orton.
Photograph by SID RHYNE.

ORTON
The Star of the Cape Fear

Orton Plantation's pastoral peace and riverside charm make it the Cape Fear River's smartest attraction. Besides the handsome plantation manor house on ancient tracts, the ruins of an aged town, what's left of the home of two royal governors, the walls of St. Philips Church, and more—are all connected by meadowlands, marshes and abandoned rice fields.

Located eighteen miles south of Wilmington just off NC 133 (follow the signs), Orton Plantation is a majestic landscape where tourists pass through to find recuperation and refreshment from their city stresses. Blessed with looks, charm and a gift of survival, Orton is the Cape Fear's hostess to the observers of an old-time rice kingdom.

This plantation seems to have been the first large rice producer on the Cape Fear River. It was first owned by Colonel Maurice Moore, who kept it a short time and then sold it to his brother Roger. In deference to Roger Moore's wealth and prestige, he was called "King Roger." King Roger's first house was destroyed by the Indians, and he, believing in "an eye for an eye," obliterated them.

King Roger built his new home at Kendal Plantation, which adjoined Orton and had also been sold to him by Colonel Maurice Moore. However, King Roger built another house at Orton, where he established his family. It has been stated that by 1735 there were substantial houses on both Orton and Kendal plantations.

Mrs. Roger Moore was a sister of Mrs. Eleazar Allen, and King Roger served with Eleazar Allen on the Council, a body of eight people of authority and influence with abundant responsibility for the proper administration of public affairs. The Eleazar Allens owned Lilliput Plantation, adjacent to Kendal. Lilliput had been granted to Allen in 1725 by Sir Thomas Frankland, the great grandson of Oliver Cromwell.

Rice was the chief crop at Orton, Kendal and Lilliput. Delancey Evans of Warrenton, Virginia, an authority on rice culture in America, says the Cape Fear River marked the northernmost limit in North America of rice culture by irrigation. So clearly defined was this northern limit, according to Evans, that the quality of rice on the south side of the Cape Fear was superior to that grown on the north side.

As Roger Moore and Eleazar Allen were considered the "chief gentlemen" of the Lower Cape Fear and their wives were sisters, one can assume that the plantations of Orton, Kendal and Lilliput were the scene of many family gatherings.

In 1757 Mr. William Hill came to the Cape Fear region, having just graduated from Harvard. Almost as soon as he laid eyes on Miss Margaret Moore, he fell in love. She, as well as her family, saw great potential in William Hill. William and Margaret were married in a beautiful wedding ceremony at Orton Plantation, which had been owned by her uncle, King Roger Moore. Margaret became a leader in the social life of that day as her husband became a prominent merchant. At a time when there was no ordained minister serving St. Philips Church, William Hill served as a lay reader and was instrumental in keeping the spiritual life of the Cape Fear alive.

The first master of Orton, King Roger Moore, had died in 1751, and according to his will, Orton Plantation and the adjacent lands "by actual survey contained 9,026 acres." An auctioneer's handbill dated August 22, 1872 revealed that this plantation contained 300 acres of superior rice land, of which 225 acres produced 16,300 bushels of rice. William's sons sold Orton to Richard Quince, a well-known merchant of Brunswick, a nearby town with a seaport.

In 1796 Richard Quince Jr. sold Orton to Benjamin Smith, a grandson of King Roger Moore. Benjamin was wealthy, gifted, and he rode high. At twenty-one he served as aide-de-camp to General Washington, and he fought with discerning perception in 1779 when the British were driven from Port Royal Sound.

In 1826 Orton Plantation was purchased by Dr. Frederick Jones Hill, a grandson of William Hill and Margaret Moore Hill. In the same manner as his grandfather, Dr. Hill was a powerhouse of community benevolences and services. He is especially remembered as being an exciting and persuasive force in the cause of a common school system. All eyes were on Orton manor house as Dr. Hill added another floor and attic and installed the famous fluted Doric columns in the style that was so popular then. Dr. Hill and his brother John, who was also a physician, owned Lilliput as well. In 1847 Dr. John Hill was buried at Orton in King Roger's burial ground.

Dr. Frederick Hill and his wife had no children, but they adopted William E. Boudinot and referred to Mrs. Hill's niece, Annie W. Davis, as their "daughter." Most of Dr. Hill's business interests were managed by a nephew, William A. Lord. Dr. Hill sold Orton Plantation in 1854, but the plantation was still in the family. Annie W. Davis was married to the new owner, Thomas C. Miller.

Title to Orton Plantation was to change hands a time or two more before the late James Sprunt bought the plantation and gave it to his wife as a gift. Sprunt was a philanthropist and the author of several books.

Sprunt encouraged his wife to enlarge the house by adding the wings to the Orton manor house. Sprunt also bought Kendal and Lilliput plantations, where the manor houses were no longer in existence. The Lilliput house had consisted of two stories and a kitchen, with necessary outbuildings and slave quarters. On November 14, 1874, the house and kitchen were destroyed by fire.

Sprunt's wife was the daughter of a former owner of Orton, Colonel K.M. Murchison. Murchison constructed a hotel in Wilmington which he named "The Orton," and it became known as the Waldorf Astoria of Wilmington. Among other Murchison enterprises in Wilmington was the Murchison National Bank.

Mrs. Sprunt, the former Luola Murchison, found one of the most unusual plantation remnants ever discovered at Orton—a man named Jeffrey Lawrence. During the Civil War, the Federals left their wounded and ill men in Orton manor house, which served as a hospital for them. They also left Jeffrey, a black man who had been a favored house servant to a distinguished Charleston family. After the war, Jeffrey remained at Orton, living alone in a small house in the woods.

Having lived and worked with the Charleston aristocracy, Jeffrey was a thoroughbred. He was tall and proud. His white hair and neatly trimmed mustache and beard emphasized his dark skin. It wasn't long before Jeffrey's tales of Charleston's blueblood society and their glorious entertainments became the fervent amusement of the Sprunts and their friends. Even the youngsters were fascinated by his stories and implored him to tell them more.

Although Jeffrey's cabin was tidy and perfectly suitable to his mode of living, Mrs. Sprunt insisted that he move to Wilmington and live in the basement of the family home. When President Taft visited the Sprunts, Jeffrey was presented to him.

For twenty years Jeffrey was sufficiently celebrated as a storyteller. One of his tales concerned the day he came upon two tiny black chimney sweeps. Jeffrey bent over in laughter as he eyed the wee black boys, covered with soot and carrying bags of the black stuff they had removed from a chimney. The small sweeps were not amused at Jeffrey's sudden emotion, and they set down their bags and threw soot on Jeffrey until he was in the same condition as they.

Orton, Kendal and Lilliput plantations are still owned by the Sprunt family. Although the manor house is private, the gardens are open to the public, and when they bloom in springtime—well, that's the most opulent period of all. Besides viewing the azaleas, camellias and faraway vistas, one can enter Luola's Chapel (at the death of his wife, Luola Murchison Sprunt, in 1916, James Sprunt had the Orton chapel built as a memorial to her), or walk among the magical blooms to the tomb of King Roger Moore. Orton Plantation is a place that's difficult to leave, but there are other sites in the vicinity worth a visit.

The remains of Brunswick Town are two miles south of Orton. Founded in 1726, this was a leading early North Carolina post. Maurice Moore contributed 320 acres for the town and King Roger added forty acres. Although there were only two streets, Bay and Second, there was a jail and a courthouse. But the town had its troubles. It was occupied by the Spanish in 1748, and there were other raids. Finally, Brunswick Town was burned by the British in 1776.

Within sight of the ruins of Brunswick Town are the ruins of St. Philip's Church and its burial ground. This structure also had its troubles. Construction was underway in 1754, but progress was slow. In July 1760, when the church construction was nearly completed, lightning struck the roof and it collapsed. When Brunswick Town was burned by the British, St. Philips probably was damaged at the same time, although the walls remain to this day.

Nearby is Russellborough, the remains of the house of royal governors Dobbs and Tryon. The house was named for its builder, Captain John Russell, commander of the British sloop *Scorpion*. Governor Arthur Dobbs bought Russellborough and lived there for about ten years, beginning in 1754. Governor William Tryon followed Dobbs, and Tryon also lived at Russellborough. When Tryon moved to New Bern, the house was bought by William Dry and the name was changed.

An especially brutal duel was fought at Russellborough. The winner wasn't satisfied with wounding his opponent with a gunshot. After the loser had been shot, he was beaten to death with the butt of the victor's pistol.

The bloodline of early Orton is not at its end, and a sense of family keeps this splendid plantation and surrounding historic sites ticking.

Russellborough, the remains of the house of royal governors Arthur Dobbs and William Tryon.
Photograhy by SID RHYNE.

The Church That Would Not Be Moved

Wachesaw Plantation is being converted into an eighteenth-century-style residential development, and the houses adjacent to the golf course are tasteful and comfortable. But if one pictures this plantation as it was when owned by Dr. Allard Belin Flagg, whose father-in-law was called the "grandee" of the rice planters, it is quite different. Flagg's wife was a daughter of Joshua John Ward of Brookgreen, and Brookgreen and Wachesaw were among the rice plantations that flourished in their prime.

The planters were galvanized by the church, for it was at church services that they met as a unit and declared their belief in God. They were inherently religious, and most of the planters attended services at All Saints Episcopal Church near Pawleys Island. Their slaves were God-fearing, heavenly-minded people, and the planters took pride in seeing that they were instructed in a moral code that involved devotional and ritual observances. A man named Albert Carolina, who was born in 1850, explained the schedule: "Brought us up in Sabbus [Sabbath]
school," he said. Sunrise prayer-meeting.
Ten o'clock Sunday school. Raise
us taughen [taught] in the church."

The earliest records show that the slaves were religious and musical beings, and their spirituals more than any other folk songs in the world are the cries of souls burdened but remembering age-old promises of eternal freedom, of feasts of milk and honey, and the divine glory of a love all-inclusive.

Although there were many slaves at Wachesaw, probably those most remembered are the Ones. There was the plantation carpenter, Michael One, Sr. and his wife Mary One, a weaver. Michael and Mary were the parents of twins, Margaret One and Michael One, Jr. Religion was an important part of the lives of the Ones and other Wachesaw slaves. "Praise Meetings" were held on this plantation, and often the slaves spoke of wanting to do something "for the Lord." In that manner they sang:

> I going to weep all I can for my Lord,
> I going to pray all I can for my Lord,
> I going to do all I can for my Lord.

The fervent prayers offered by the slaves became an inspiration to all who heard them. One old soul said, "Lord, we are nothing but graveyard travelers and the twinkling of a mother's dust."

Another of the faithful, praying for the minister, said, "Go with the speaker. Bless him. Go with the one what stand in John shoe. Help him to tell men the wages of sin death, and the gift of God eternal life. Have mercy on him if You so please."

It was during 1854 that a definite change seized the planters who lived in the northern region of the parish. They complained that the journey to All Saints Church was too arduous and the distance too far to travel. It wasn't the easiest thing in the world to lumber down the dusty, gutted road in their carriages, or travel by boat for many miles in order to reach that place of worship. As the planters talked about it, they decided they could no longer put up with the long distance those who lived in the northern part of the parish had to travel. It was agreed that they would talk with church officials about building a small church in their vicinity.

At first they got nowhere in their sales presentation, and they seemed unhappy. Finally they decided to push even harder for a church nearer their plantations.

After a meeting in which the planters had strongly petitioned for a church in their area, on December 24, 1854 the vestry resolved to build a church at Wachesaw Plantation. A building committee was appointed.

The cornerstone was laid on April 11, 1855. On the east side the inscription read:

> In the name of the Father
> The Son and the Holy Ghost
> Amen

The Right Revd. T. F. Davis, D.D.
Bishop of South Carolina
Laid This As the Corner Stone of
A Building Dedicated to the Worship of
Almighty God
According to the Rites of the Protestant
Episcopal Church Under the Name of
Saint John the Evangelist
On the 11 day of April MDCCCLV

On the north side:

Rector of All Saints Parish
The Revd. Alexander Glennie, A.M.
Assistant Minister
The Revd. Lucien Charles Lance, B.A.
Building Committee
Francis W. Heriot
Plowden C. J. Weston
Allard B. Flagg
Glory Be to God on High and on Earth
Peace Good Will Toward Men

The new church, which was called "a chapel of ease," was named Saint John the Evangelist, and the communion silver was engraved with that name. The chapel consisted of eighteen pews, thirteen of which sold for $100 each. There were sixteen benches for the use of favorite slaves.

Through the years Saint John the Evangelist was the fundamental strength of the planters in the Murrells Inlet area. But the vitality of the church began to fall when the Civil War began. By the end of the war, the strength of the church was decidedly down, and the planters were in trauma as they tried to reorganize their plantations and pick up their lives again. The planters looked on the little chapel as a symbol of happier times, and when the structure began to weaken, seemingly in spirit as well as from decay, its owner, Dr. Allard Belin Flagg of Wachesaw, made plans to dismantle the building and use the materials to construct a beach house.

The freedmen who were still working at Wachesaw followed

the instructions of Dr. Flagg, but they warned him that it was wrong to make a house from a church. They were rugged Christians, and they believed this perfectly. However, Dr. Flagg did not believe that the outlook for his beach house was so grave, and he went ahead with the construction of the house, which was being built entirely of materials taken from the dilapidated church.

Almost at the moment that the last board was attached to the cottage on the seashore portion of the plantation, a violent storm crashed ashore. Storms were not strangers to this part of the coast, for South Carolina is on the northwestern edge of a major corridor of hurricane activity. The first recorded tropical storm to hit along this coast was in August 1686, but the Indians had told the early settlers of a tremendous hurricane during which water rose over the tops of trees. So many hurricanes had brought destruction to this coast that a poem regarding the likeliest time for a savage storm to hit the area was making the rounds:

> June, too soon
> July, stand by
> August, come it must
> September, remember
> October, all over

The fast-moving storm that hit the little house made from a church was here and gone in eighteen hours. The beach house was in shambles, and former slaves were careful not to let an I-told-you-so smile spread over their lips.

Dr. Flagg was a disappointed but determined man. In his black suit and hat, he towered over his workers. Although they strenuously objected, he said he still believed that from the wreckage could emerge another beach house. In a new-found aggressiveness and responsiveness, he put the workers back to work, building the beach house. Although they again warned him that a house could not be made from a church, Dr. Flagg didn't believe their grim prediction. Instead, the planter remained fundamentally positive and passed off the warning as silly superstition. But just as the house was ready for occupancy, another hurricane arrived. This storm was not a start-and-stop one. It hit the shore traveling at more than fifty miles per hour. During the next few hours it became a towering monster, and when the calm, quiet eye of the storm arrived, those who were brave enough to venture to the seashore for a look discovered that many beach cottages had been washed to sea, including the house that had been made from a church. When the other side of the eye of the storm smashed the shore, it was even more devastating that the first side of the circular demon.

Copy of Portrait of Theodosia Burr *(Mrs. Joseph Alston), oil on canvas, John Vanderlyn (American, 1775–1852).*

Courtesy of Yale University Art Gallery.
Gift of Oliver Burr Jennings in memory of Annie Burr Jennings.

The Tale Of The Oaks

The Oaks Plantation is one of the plantations acquired by Archer Milton Huntington when he bought four plantations in order to create Brookgreen Gardens. Although few people walk into the forest to view the family cemetery which is the only remnant of a once-prosperous rice plantation on the Waccamaw River, one of the most poignant stories of the Low Country came from this place.

Young Joseph Alston, who had inherited The Oaks and was to own two elegant Charleston townhouses, was visiting relatives who lived on the Hudson River in New York when he met and fell in love with Theodosia Burr, the only child of Aaron Burr. Theodosia had red hair, and Washington Irving, essayist and historian, said that when she danced, other dancers went to the sidelines to watch her graceful movements. In some ways Theodosia and Joseph were alike. The both had brilliant minds and were eager to study and improve themselves any way they could.

Burr fretted over the love affair of his daughter and the young man from South Carolina. Should she marry this man, Theodosia would not live the life he had envisioned for her. With her physical attributes and training, she could become a titled woman, a queen or a princess. Burr had lavished all his love on his daughter from the time of his wife's death in 1794, and he had tutored her in foreign languages, philosophy and the theories of economics. At sixteen, Theodosia spoke six languages. The last place in the world she could show off her linguistic knowledge would be on a Low Country plantation. He must, and he *would,* he declared, do anything in his power to prevent the occurrence of a marriage between his daughter and Joseph Alston of South Carolina.

After he returned to South Carolina, Joseph feared Theodosia would be influenced by her father, and wrote in an effort to impress her with his education, good manners and wealth. It must not be overlooked, he wrote, that he had finished the study for practicing law at the bar before he was twenty. And having inherited The Oaks Plantation from his grandfather, he was a wealthy man. Joseph assured Theodosia in the letter that he was a man of superior refinement, having attended Princeton and traveled widely, and with his resources he had little to do with the drudgery of the business of running the plantation.

Theodosia was not swayed by her father's rejection of Joseph, and she continued to recount the good qualities of her friend. But Burr was a man hard to convince. He was excited over politics and at that time Joseph had shown no interest in government. Burr found this trait distasteful, and he continued to be annoyed over the relationship.

Finally Theodosia convinced her father that Joseph was the love of her life; Burr relented and gave his consent. The lavish wedding was held in Albany, New York in February 1801.

Soon after Joseph took Theo south, Aaron Burr became Vice President of the United States. (He had wanted to become President!) The bride and groom traveled from their plantation to Washington City, the nation's new capital. They wanted to be in attendance at the inauguration ceremonies of President Thomas Jefferson and Vice President Burr.

There were no inns in Washington City, and it was necessary for Burr to take refuge in a dreary rooming house. Theodosia and Joseph visited friends who lived in Virginia.

Theo's friends, who now had an opportunity to observe her after her wedding, watched her carefully. They looked for some indication of whether or not she was happy on the plantation in the South. They had heard that Georgetown County was a remote place. It was no secret that the plantation on the Waccamaw River was heavy with cypress, pine and oak trees, all veiled in Spanish moss. Darkness fell early at The Oaks, and after dark the moss brought an eeriness as it silvered in the glint of the moon. Alligators bellowed between midnight and daybreak, and hurricanes swept ashore on the Atlantic's tides just a mile or two to the east. If she were not happy in her role as Joseph Alston's wife, Theo gave no hint of it. But she was concerned for her father, who still felt she had married "beneath her station in life."

Burr urged Joseph to cultivate his daughter's mind in order to keep her occupied, and he insisted that his son-in-law acquire a knowledge of Latin and all branches of philosophy.

Theodosia and Joseph endured all of Burr's sentiments and in May 1803 his doubts and fears were swept away by the happiness he attained when Theodosia gave birth to a son—Aaron Burr Alston. Burr was so thrilled with the announcement of the arrival of his grandson that he gave a glittering party. Dolley Madison, the wife of future President James Madison, said Burr carried on too expansively over his grandson. "You would think no one else ever had a grandson," she said. Aaron Burr Alston was nicknamed Gampy. The family was ecstatically happy and in March 1804 moved into a new home at The Oaks.

Little is known of this house, except that it was described as being very "elaborate." Theo had a servant to attend to every task, but at this time her health began to fail. She wrote to her father:

> Ever since the date of my last letter, I have been quite ill. . . . I was one night so ill as to have lost my senses in a great measure; about daylight, as a last resource, they began plying me with old wine, and blisters to my feet. But, on recovering a little, I kicked off the blisters, and declared I would be dressed; carried in the open air, and have free use of cold water. I was indulged.

Theo's health went into sharp descent, and it further declined when she learned that her father had killed Alexander Hamilton in a duel with pistols. She was in a kind of stupor over all of this. It was during this time that her husband was taking his father-in-law's advice and making a name for himself in South Carolina politics. He was elected Speaker of the House, generally the most influential office in the state, as committees influencing the flow of legislation were under his control.

Unfortunately, Theo was now realizing that as a New Yorker she had not been bred for the outdoor life as had the more sturdy members of her husband's family. As the years passed, she became even more frail. Her condition was not helped when she learned that her father had become engaged in what was called a "conspiracy." Word had come to her that her father contrived a plan to head an expedition against Mexico, believing there would be a war between the United States and that country. Theo vehemently aided her father in an effort to confirm his innocence, and Joseph wrote a report stating that the conspiracy was founded on innuendo. But the biggest blow that Theo was to endure was still to come.

The weather in South Carolina was humid, and her mental and physical health were deteriorating. She may have begun to worry about the treatment she was receiving when Joseph was away attending to his political duties. What medical treatment was being administered to her? she wondered. She had learned that the slaves had brought with them from Africa a strong tendency toward belief in witchcraft. The older and more crafty slaves possessed some skill in healing as well as poisonous plants which well qualified them for imposition upon the weak, and Theodosia felt that she was easily imposed upon.

Some of the "healers" used what they called "conjur bags." These consisted of cotton cloth holding ashes and salt, dirt from a grave and a few hairs yanked from the head of the ailing person; these magic bags were believed to have healing qualities. Mashed onions were sometimes placed on the neck as a cure, or a nutmeg on a string was hung around one's neck. There were other peculiar "cures" that may have passed into and out of Theo's thinking. But Joseph had seen to it that she was receiving the best care the Low Country had to offer.

Finally, as Theodosia wilted in the heat, Joseph suggested that they take their son and go to the family home on Debordieu Island, the seashore property under their ownership. They would enjoy the cool sea breezes and take frequent dips in the ocean.

Moving over to the beach house was a chore, as so many items had to be moved. Bedding, food, books—everything they would need was finally packed. When they arrived at Debordieu, the sky and sea were glorious. Soon Theodosia's condition improved, but her pleasure was interrupted when her son took a head cold. Joseph sent for not one but several physicians, who were on the scene as soon as possible for those days. Their diagnoses revealed that the boy had the dreaded malarial fever. Within hours he was dead, and Theo's world crashed around her. She weakly lifted her pen and wrote to Burr: "My dear father. . . . there is no more joy for me, the world is a blank. I have lost my boy. My child is gone forever. He expired on the 30th of June."

Theo went into seclusion, and her father was in a frenzy over her poor health. He wrote to her and insisted she come to New York for a visit with him. Theo now had reached her lowest state of dejection. In her worsening health, it came to her that perhaps she should not have come to South Carolina to live. She wondered if her father and her friends had been correct in their presumption that she just wasn't up to living in the coastal area of the South.

Joseph was now governor of South Carolina, and he made preparations for Theodosia to go to New York. On the day the vessel was to sail, Joseph accompanied his young wife from The Oaks Plantation to Georgetown. They walked down the old Rice Island Steps at Brookgreen and boarded a small vessel that took them on the outgoing tide to Georgetown. *The Patriot* was not ready to sail, and Theo and her husband and servants waited in a brick building. They heard talk of pirates and also of a violent storm at sea. Finally the vessel was ready to go, and Theodosia, along with her servants, walked to the dock and on to the ship. She was wearing a silk dress trimmed in lace and carrying her sewing basket.

After pulling away from the dock, *The Patriot* headed out into the Atlantic. The ship was laden with casks of rice to defray expenses, and the first officer had in his possession a letter written by Governor Alston to the British Admiral off the Capes, advising that his wife was on broad and requesting permission for a passage through the fleet.

Aaron Burr kept vigil in the port of New York, waiting for the arrival of *The Patriot*. He couldn't wait to throw his arms around his beloved daughter. She was so dear to him that he believed he would never get over her marriage and move to South Carolina. As he thought about it, he pictured the reunion. He would hug her, then hold her back and observe her, and then hug her again. Her health would be restored after she arrived in New York, the place he believed to be her real home. Home, he thought, home. Theo was coming home. But the vessel failed to arrive at the expected time. Burr continued to wait and watch for *The Patriot*. He interrupted busy dockhands and shiphands and passengers and officers of other vessels, asking if they knew the whereabouts of *The Patriot*. None of them had the remotest idea of the location of the ship.

Burr sent word to Joseph that the ship bearing Theo had failed to arrive. Joseph was devastated, and he immediately instituted a search. All the people of South Carolina were concerned. Where *was* the frail young wife of their governor?

The search continued, but there was no word anywhere on the fate of *The Patriot*. Finally, Joseph Alston and Aaron Burr came to the conclusion that *The Patriot* and all hands had been lost at sea. The two men, one in New York and the other in South Carolina, endeavored to accept their loss. Newspapers still carried accounts of the disappearance of South Carolina's First Lady, and there were rumors. One story said that pirates had overtaken the ship and forced "the white lady" to walk the plank. Another story reported that the vessel had been smashed to splinters in a hurricane.

Joseph Alston died in 1816, at the age of thirty-seven. His estate passed by his will to his brothers, John Ashe Alston and William Algernon Alston. Joseph's remains were laid to rest alongside his son's, in the Alston Family Cemetery at The Oaks Plantation.

Some years later, a newspaper account revealed the confessions of a pirate who said he had seen Theo being forced to "walk the plank." This story was generally believed, until an account emerged of a physician who had treated a sick woman on North Carolina's Outer Banks.

The patient had no funds with which to pay the physician for medical services, and she offered him a portrait which she believed was a picture of the late Theodosia Burr Alston. The patient explained that some years earlier a schooner had washed ashore after a hurricane. A family named Tillett found the craft and examined it. In one of the cabins, scattered about the floor were dresses of silk, trimmed in lace. Lying among the debris was a sewing basket, and a portrait of a lovely young woman had fallen from a wall. The Tillett family had taken the sewing basket, but the portrait had come into the possession of the patient. She gave it to the physician.

The physician, realizing that other portraits of Theodosia Burr Alston had been painted, searched for a likeness to compare to the one he now owned. Finally such a portrait was located. When the two were compared, the painting held by the physician appeared to be of the very same woman.

From The Seed Of An Ear Of Rice A Millionaire Is Made

Hundreds of statues stand in eerie silence. Sunlight, shafting through the branches of ancient trees, glints on bronze and marble, while other statues are shaded, set in niches along ivy-covered brick walls.

Brookgreen Gardens, on US 17 south of Murrells Inlet near Litchfield, is an outdoor museum devoted to displaying sculpture and preserving traces of the events and people that contributed to the history of one of the outstanding Waccamaw River plantations. The unspoiled setting seems perfect for a plantation and an outdoor museum.

Brookgreen manor house was built by William Allston, a son of John Allston who came to the area known today as the S.C. Grand Strand early in the eighteenth century. But this story is about Joshua John Ward. He was born at Brookgreen on November 24, 1800, a son of Major Joshua Ward of Charleston.

At the age of 25, Joshua John married Joanna Douglas Hasell, a daughter of G.P.B. Hasell of Edinburgh, and they had two sons and eight daughters. Under Ward's stewardship, Brookgreen reached its zenith of prosperity. (He consistently reinvested his assets in more land and slaves.) In addition to Brookgreen, Ward acquired Prospect Hill, Alderly, Rose Hill and Oryzantia plantations. He saw to it that every available inch of land bordering the Waccamaw was cleared of stumps and trees, and he installed a system of levees, drains and gates that governed the flooding of the fields. He was the dominant rice planter of the Waccamaw peninsula in that day.

But just as important as labor or land in Ward's success was the discovery of a high-yield strain called "big grain rice." Joshua John Ward wrote a letter on November 1, 1843 in which he said:

> In 1838, my overseer, Mr. James C. Thompson, a very judicious planter, residing on my Brook Green estate, accidentally discovered in the barnyard during the threshing season a part of an ear of rice, from the peculiarity of which he was induced to preserve it, until he had an interview with me.

The seed from this ear of rice was planted in 1840 and yielded forty-nine bushels. The following year the seed rice was sown in a field of twenty-one acres and yielded 1,170 bushels.

In 1850 Ward produced 3,900,000 pounds of rice with the help of his slaves. During these years there was always plenty of domestic help, and food for the Brookgreen table was more than ample. Also in 1850, from the Ward gardens came 7,000 bushels of corn, 2,000 bushels of oats, 1,000 bushels of peas and beans, and 66,000 bushels of sweet potatoes.

Joshua Ward, a millionaire in a day when millionaires were rare

Original kitchen used when Joshua John Ward, millionaire rice planter, owned Brookgreen Gardens. The boxwoods are also from the Ward days. Courtesy Brookgreen Gardens.

indeed, died in 1853. Some of his children had not come of age. To his eldest son Joshua he left Brookgreen, and this Joshua Ward, in the tradition of his father, continued the cultivation of rice.

Joanna Hasell Ward bought the house at 635 East Bay Street in Charleston that had been built by Henry and Joseph Faber in the 1830s. Although the house at Brookgreen was not a grand manor house, Joanna's Charleston house had been compared with the Villa Malcontenta at Brentna, Italy, designed by Andrea Palladio, an architect of the sixteenth century. The house had a portico set on a fifteen-foot high terrace of arches, and the portico roof was supported by four Ionic columns. There was a marble mantel in each room, and the mahogany doors had pewter handles. A spiral stairway rose from the ground floor to the hexagonal cupola on the top. The staircase of mahogany had massive carved newel posts and tapering balusters. The house faced east, overlooking the Cooper and Wando rivers.

Although the widow Ward spent most of her time in Charleston, she kept in touch with her son and his family at Brookgreen, where the ear of rice had been discovered in the stableyard.

Joanna Ward's Charleston house at 635 East Bay Street. Today the house is used for business enterprises, but it can be viewed on the exterior.
Photograph by SID RHYNE.

Diana of the Chase, by Anna Hyatt Huntington. Diana was placed in one of the niches in the dining room of the Huntington home at 1083 Fifth Avenue, New York City before being moved to Brookgreen.
Courtesy of Brookgreen Gardens.

Mrs. Huntington's Ninetieth Birthday

Although it was her ninetieth birthday, the day started much like any other for Anna Hyatt Huntington. Her arthritis was a nuisance, but she still was able to put in at least three hours a day on her sculpture. She was also still capable of girlish delight and entered into projects with enthusiasm. She was quick to laugh, even at herself, and she got a kick out of remembering that movie actor Cesar Romero came to the New York dedication of her statue of Cuban liberator Jose Marti, Romero's grandfather.

"The women gasped," Mrs. Huntington remarked. "They said, 'ooh, ooh,' when he stood next to me!"

The twenty-room mansion on Sunset Road in Redding, Connecticut smelled of damp clay on her ninetieth birthday, just as always. But the day wouldn't remain tranquil for the woman who, along with her husband, had created Brookgreen Gardens near Murrells Inlet.

In 1930 there were hunger marches in England, and the United States was in the throes of the Great Depression. In that same year a yacht, *The Rocinante,* sailing en route to the West Indies, docked at Georgetown. Before the vessel left, its owner, Archer Milton Huntington, had made plans to buy four adjoining plantations, including Brookgreen.

Huntington's father, Collis P. Huntington, had built the Central Pacific Railroad and had been counted one of the twelve richest men in the country. He owned fabulous houses on Nob Hill in San Francisco and on Fifth Avenue in New York, as well as a camp in the Adirondack Mountains. A shrewd pennypincher, Collis Huntington had said that he would not be traced by the quarters he dropped, nor would he be remembered for the money he gave away. He left $60 million when he died at seventy-nine, not knowing that one day his son Archer would give away more than $50 million, much of it to museums.

When Archer Huntington bought Brookgreen and the other plantations, he also acquired enough land to round out 10,000 acres. His interest each day on his investments was believed to amount to $80,000. He gave Anna $10 million "to play with" as she designed a garden for her statuary and the works of other artists. She designed the plantation/museum in the shape of a butterfly's wings.

Mrs. Huntington had the help of some of the best carpenters in the area, including Welcome Beese. Beese was known as the strongest man on the Waccamaw Neck. According to the late Edwin O. Fulton, his wrists testified to his strength, as they were much larger and thicker than normal wrists. One day, as Beese stood on the loading platform at a country store, a load of bags of salt, weighing 200 pounds each, arrived. Someone promised him that if he could carry three of the bags into the store at one time, he would receive as a reward a jar of whiskey. Beese put one bag under one arm and another bag under the other arm; then he lifted the third bag with his teeth and carried the 600 pounds of salt into the store.

On another occasion, Welcome Beese was arrested for non-payment of poll taxes. He was handcuffed and put into a patrol car. After they had traveled several miles from Brookgreen, he stretched his wrists and broke the handcuffs, then hit the driver on the head and knocked him out.

As Beese neared his 100th birthday, Mrs. Huntington asked him what he wanted as a present. He told her that he would like to see his tombstone and have it engraved. She put in a call to Georgetown and had the stone engraved with his name and year of birth, 1833. The stone stands at Welcome Beese's gravesite in a cemetery adjacent to US 17, near Pawley's Island. The date of his death, March 1942, was never cut into the stone.

Archer Huntington died on December 11, 1955 at age eighty-six. His obituary noted that he had given away much of his multi-million-dollar fortune in founding and supporting museums.

Anna Hyatt Huntington spent her last years at her home in Connecticut. (She died in 1973, at the age of ninety-seven.) Every birthday was special to her, and she usually greeted her nephew, niece and friends in a "family gathering." But as the day of her ninetieth birthday progressed, flowers began to arrive. She had finished her work for the day and sat down among the flowers and glanced at the portraits on the wall, likenesses of her late husband and father-in-law. But her reverie wasn't to last for long. People began to arrive to wish her happy birthday, and messages from important people from around the world came—all at once.

Birthday messages arrived from President Johnson, Vice President Humphrey, Governor Dempsey, the chief executives of other states, and various political figures. By the time the day had ended, more than 200 people had come to Mrs. Huntington's home to wish her well. She graciously received each of them, and when the day came to an end, the ninety-year-old sculptress looked as fresh as when it started.

"When this is all over, she'll be the least tired person here," a friend remarked.

Mrs. Huntington's energy belied her reply to the question of how she liked being ninety.

"I don't like to be ninety," she answered. "I'd rather be in my seventies when I could do more. My joints didn't creak then."

Mrs. Huntington, at age 94, in her studio. The sculpture of the man with arm extended is that of her father-in-law, Collis P. Huntington.
Photograph by Laurence Willard for YANKEE Magazine.

THE REVEREND ALEXANDER GLENNIE by Charles Fraser.
Courtesy of the Carolina Art Association, Gibbes Art Gallery.

The Unforgettable Dr. Glennie

To walk among the oaks and cedars in the burial ground of All Saints Church, Waccamaw, on SC 255 about three miles west of Pawley's Island, is to discover the extraordinary rice planters who made the history of this coastal land from antebellum times. Moss swings from an oak limb and brushes a marble stone in memory of Thomas George and Mary Allston Pawley. He donated about twenty acres for All Saints Church and cemetery. A few steps from that grave marker is the resting place of Plowden C.J. Weston, a planter noted for his wealth and literary and social qualities. According to the words on the stone, Weston "fell asleep on January 25, 1864 at age forty-four."

The early rectors endeavored to serve their widely-scattered people as best they could in a parish that was cut off from the mainland by water except to the north. The Waccamaw River flows in the same general direction described by the line of the South Carolina coast, draining into Winyah Bay at Georgetown along with the Pee Dee, Black and Sampit rivers. When the Colonial Assembly passed an act creating the Parish of All Saints, the parish included the whole of the Waccamaw peninsula, which is about thirty miles in length and varying from two to three miles in width.

Faithful members had to travel by carriage on dusty, rutted roadways, or by boat on the Waccamaw River and then nearly a mile on Chapel Creek, which led from the river to the All Saints landing. Attending services was more or less an all-day affair. Food from the plantations was taken along to provide for Sunday meals, which were eaten in the churchyard after services.

During its early years there the parish had one rector after another. It seemed the rectors didn't favor serving in so remote a place. Some of the rectors began planting rice after they realized the enormous profits from rice production.

In 1829, Francis Marion Weston, a wealthy planter who owned Laurel Hill and Hagley plantations, brought Alexander Glennie from England to tutor his son Plowden. In short order, Glennie proclaimed that Plowden was prepared to study in England, and his parents took him there and enrolled him at Harrow. Glennie was asked to become rector of All Saints. His work began as a lay reader and then he was admitted as a candidate for Holy Orders. He was made deacon by the Bishop in 1832, and on February 13, 1833 he was ordained a priest.

Dr. Glennie established his authority largely through the power of his personality. Virtually everyone who met him, black as well as white, found him dignified and magnetic.

The church was not large enough to serve the local slave population, which at some plantations numbered in the hundreds. Glennie came to believe that the lack of spiritual attention to the slaves was an abomination to the Lord. Most of them, he learned, were inherently religious, and they possessed exceptional gifts of harmony. Many of their songs, sermons, prayers and thoughts were on heaven. One woman was said to "pitch" her song of heaven:

> Oh, what are they doing in heaven today?
> Where sins in sorrow is all done away!
> And peace above like a river they say,
> Oh, what are they doing there now?

And another woman gave her conception of heaven:

> Hebben be a beautiful place. The streets all lined with gold, diamonds and pearls. If you is faithful enough to get there! There's twelve gates and two angels at every gate. An angel will take you and wash you good, dress you up in fine clothes, and put six wings on you. . . . Then the angel comes and takes you up the street called Hallelujah Street. Then they takes you to Amen Street. Then while you're flying and you're so happy you'll be singing.

Often the adult slaves spoke of wanting to do something "for the Lord." In that manner, they sang:

I going to weep all I can for my Lord,
I going to pray all I can for my Lord,
I going to do all I can for my Lord.

The slaves attended what they called "praise meetings" or "shouts" in their cabins. Dr. Glennie found this practice not to his liking, as he believed that every person should have access to a chapel or church. Glennie rode his horse to every plantation in his parish and persuaded the planters to build chapels. Soon construction was begun on small clapboard chapels for the slaves. Dr. Glennie visited the plantations once each month and instructed the slaves and their children. He was especially loved and respected by the children.

Glennie's role as the spiritual leader of the slave children was momentous. Until his death he was the man revered by the parish as the founder of the religious education of slave children. Although his sermons were simple, they were eloquent.

All Saints Church near Pawleys Island.
Photograph by SID RHYNE.

> Christ Jesus came into the world. Where did He come from? Every tongue is ready to say He came down from heaven. He said to his disciples, 'I came forth from the Father.' We read of Him, in the Holy Bible, as the Son of God: the same yesterday, and today, and forever, without beginning and without end, the mighty God. He is one with the Father and the Holy Ghost. From this state of glory and majesty did He come, when He came into the world to save sinners. What love ought we sinners to feel towards Him! And how ready should we be to shew our love to Him by a willing obedience! But in what condition did he come? Did He appear in the world in a state of great power and glory? No. It is written *the Word was made flesh, and dwelt among us.* God was manifest in the flesh. He who was God, made himself no reputation, and took upon him the form of a servant, and was made in the likeness of men. You see how low our Lord Jesus Christ stooped when he came to save sinners? He that was the Lord, in heaven, took the nature of man on earth. And he did not appear as a great and rich man, but He took the form of a servant. When born of his virgin mother, He was laid in a manager. He spent all His days in a state of poverty. When going about preaching his gospel, he said of Himself, *the Son of Man hath not where to lay His head.* And you know what sorrow of soul, what pain of body, he endured. It is not amazing that the Lord from heaven should bring Himself down so low as this, that He might save lost sinners. Oh, if you feel this as you ought to do, the love of Christ will constrain you, not only to trust in Him as your Saviour, but also to be obedient to Him as your Lord and Master.

After the plantation owners learned the rites of the service, they often held services for their slaves without the help of Glennie.

Bishop Philander Chase, a famous missionary bishop of the Midwest, came to the parish and visited the plantations and All Saints Church. "The black children of a South Carolina planter know more of Christianity than thousands of white children in Illinois," he said.

The Stubborn Bottle Of Wine

The earliest record of Litchfield Plantation is a plat showing the division of the property at the death of Peter Simons in 1794; the map shows the same house and avenue of live oaks that are there today.

This Waccamaw River mansion, near Pawleys Island, with its courtyards, terraces, gardens and carriage house, resembles a European village. Although the opulence and gracious living of the rice planters is over, this plantation provides a graphic idea of what it was like.

Peter Simons left Litchfield to his son John, who sold it to Daniel Tucker of the Bermudas. Litchfield's Daniel Tucker was a member of Georgetown's Committee of Safety during the Revolution, and his plantation was well known during his years of ownership, as he remained active in political affairs. When Daniel Tucker died in 1797, he left Litchfield to his three sons, John Hyrne, Daniel and George Tucker.

In his later years, John Hyrne became the sole owner. Although he married four times, he was said to have a shocking face, deeply pitted by smallpox scars. Additionally, he had an enormous blue-veined nose with what appeared to be a cauliflower cluster on the end.

John Hyrne Tucker graduated from Brown University in the class of 1800 and married Fannie Caroline Brown of Georgetown. They had no children. Fannie died in 1806. Tucker's second wife was Elizabeth Ann Allston, a sister of Robert F.W. Allston, who became a governor of South Carolina. Elizabeth Ann and John had two daughters, Elizabeth and Anne. John Hyrne's last two wives were the Ramsay sisters, Susan and Martha, nieces of

Litchfield Plantation manor house.
Photograph by SID RHYNE.

David Ramsay, who wrote an early history of South Carolina. Martha was Tucker's last wife, and she bore no children, but Susan, the third wife, had seven.

A Charlestonian, Frederick Adolphus Porcher (POOR-shay), wrote in his memoirs that Tucker had an exquisite taste in wines. He had a large stock of the best Madeira and was almost as proud of his wine as of his crops.

Although John Tucker was religious almost to the point of fanaticism, regarding the Episcopal Church as the only true and safe road to heaven, according to Porcher, he enjoyed the sociability of clubs. He was especially convivial when he attended functions at the Pee Dee Club, established by a group of planters for purposes of companionship. Sumptuous meals were served at the club, after which the planters discussed the latest news from England and the newer skills and techniques in agriculture. Tucker figured in one story concerning the Pee Dee Club.

Martin Van Buren, after his term as President of the United States, was present at a dinner at the Pee Dee Club one night when John Tucker was presiding. As Tucker stood before the people gathered there, he lifted a bottle of wine and called it to the former President's attention. Van Buren leaned forward and scrutinized the wine. As Tucker talked about the bouquet and elegance of the wine, speaking in superlatives, he said it lacked for nothing. But all the while he was trying to pull the cork from the bottle. He pulled mightily, but the cork remained stuck. Finally, Tucker pulled with all the strength he could muster. His face turned red, veins stood out on his neck, and he clenched his teeth together as he pulled. Then, unexpectedly, the cork flew from the bottle with such force that it struck a blow on Tucker's cauliflower nose. Blood trickled down his chin and dropped onto his clothing. A guest pulled a patch of fur from his hat, ran to the head table, and stuck the fur on the knob of Tucker's nose. The fur restrained the bleeding, and the master of ceremonies, fur attached to his nose, continued to preside at the meeting as though nothing had happened.

The Pelican Inn at Pawleys Island. This was the beach house of Plowden C.J. Weston of Hagley Plantation.
Photograph by SID RHYNE.

The Feast of Company A

Hagley Plantation was once a *grande dame* of plantation life. In its heyday, there were lavish dinners, with porcelain dishes and rare wines served in crystal imported from England. Located on a bend in the Waccamaw River between Pawley's Island and Georgetown, Hagley is nearer to the ocean than some other plantations, such as Brookgreen and Litchfield. Here powerful tides still flood the fields that once produced vast quantities of rice.

Francis Marion Weston, who inherited Laurel Hill Plantation from his father, bought Hagley in 1837. Francis had married a first cousin, Mildred Weston, from Warwickshire, England. On August 21, 1819, while they were visiting in England, a son, Plowder Charles Jennet Weston was born. Mildred died three years later, and Francis married her sister Mary. When they were not in Europe, the family lived at Laurel Hill.

When Plowden Weston was old enough to begin his schooling, Alexander Glennie was brought from Europe to tutor him. In 1831 the young man was enrolled at Harrow. Plowden studied fine arts and wrote a poem entitled "The Pleasures of Music" which was published in England. The poem was dedicated to his good friend and classmate, William Clement Drake Esdaile. In it the student wrote of his home in South Carolina:

> And wished I could recall the dreams
> I saw,
> Stretched on the banks, romantic Waccamaw!
> Thus have I wandered, thus, thy coasts along,
> While Carolina echoed with my song.

When Plowden finished his work at Harrow, he attended Cambridge.

On August 31, 1847 Plowden Weston married Emily Frances Esdaile, a sister of his Harrow classmate, and the young couple sailed for Hagley Plantation to establish a home, although the title to the plantation was still in his father's name.

Hagley Plantation manor house was about seventy-five feet in length, with a passageway running the entire length. On one side of the hall, according to a contemporary account, were the dining room and drawing rooms, all with connecting doors. On the other side of the passageway was Weston's library, which consisted of several rooms containing books valued at over $15,000. Many of the books were bound in brown and red leather, with colored illustrations. Classics by ancient Greek and Roman writers, as well as English literature, were well represented. There was also a huge Bible. The mansion was about a "five minutes walk from the boat landing," according to Elizabeth Collins, who came from England to visit the Westons. Trees surrounded the house, and an orange tree shaded the kitchen.

It was a rule of the Westons to visit England every other year so that Emily could spend time with members of her family. She had a clear soprano voice, and she always sang happily as she made plans to go home.

Sometime prior to 1858, Weston had a house built on the seashore at Pawley's Island. It stood between the All Saints Church summer rectory and the summer home of the Allstons. The beach house was built by Renty, a clever and artistic slave whom the Westons had sent to England to learn cabinetry and the building of fine structures. The beach house was built of cypress, which was called "the everlasting wood," as it was believed to be a near-perfect wood. Roman numerals were carved in the beams and boards after they were hewn on the plantation, and when the materials reached the island, Weston's workers, following the numerals, placed the boards and beams in their proper positions. They were then fastened together with pegs of wood.

Elizabeth Collins said the beach house was "lofty," and one could enjoy cool breezes in any part of the building. As there were frequently heavy storms on this island, the Weston house was struck by lightning many times, but little damage was done.

Plowden Weston became noted for his wealth and his vast knowledge of many subjects, as well as his unusual ability as a public speaker. He was a member of the Hot and Hot Fish Club and the Planters Club, both formed for the conviviality of the planters. When he was invited to speak before the Winyah Indigo Society in Georgetown, he took as his subject the works of the authors and poets he had studied. He began his speech by quoting from the first essay written by Francis Bacon, and also mentioned his respect for the writings of Carlyle, Ruskin and Tennyson.

Weston's house servants included Hector, the head servant; Prince, the coachman; Caesar, Jack and Gabriel, the footmen; Rachel, the washerwoman; Josephine and Dolly, who were seamstresses; Phyllis and Susanne, the cooks; and Mary, the housemaid. Prince, the coachman, was the principal fiddler; he also played tambourine and banjo. His favorite tunes were *Dixie Land* and country dance tunes.

Most of Weston's slaves had been born on the plantation, but one, slave "Old Pembra," had been born in Africa. According to slave reminiscences that have been preserved, slaves from other plantations went to her for cures.

On December 10, 1860 the Ordinance of Secession was passed. South Carolina was divided into ten military districts, and each district was to furnish a company of men. The Georgetown Rifle Guards were the first to be organized, and Weston became a private in the guards. He fed the company from his own provisions, and the meals were feasts—hams from the smokehouse, turkeys from the fowl pens, champagne from the cellar. He also provided 150 Enfield rifles which he had ordered from England, and military uniforms. Four of his slaves served as a military band, as the fifer and drummers led the way for the Georgetown Rifle Guards.

After a few months, the Georgetown Rifle Guards became Company A of the Tenth South Carolina Regiment, serving under Colonel Arthur Middleton Manigault. Plowden Weston was unanimously elected Captain of Company A.

Emily Weston missed her husband terribly. One day she decided to travel to the camp to visit him. While she was away, an enemy vessel came close to the plantation and the sounds of heavy cannon thundered over Hagley. A frightened slave petitioned, "Please Master Jesus, save me!" The ship left after a few hours, but it was evident that all was not safe on the plantation.

One day in 1861, word came that the enemy was landing troops along the Waccamaw River! Colonel Manigault rounded up Company A along with some other units and rushed to the site of the conflict. But when the men reached the supposedly threatened place, all was quiet. To compensate for the wasted trip, Captain Weston invited all the soldiers to Hagley for a meal. According to a slave's account, Weston sent no advance word that 150 men were coming for dinner. After their arrival at Hagley, in just under three hours, the entire party was seated at tables set up in Weston's dining room and drawing room, which had connecting doors. The men feasted on turkey, duck, rice, vegetables, pastries, bread and wines. It was a legendary banquet for Company A.

The President On The Carpet

Arcadia Plantation house and gardens are private, but for two days each spring (in late March or early April) the gardens are usually opened to the public. This happens during the annual plantation tour sponsored by the women of the Church of Prince George Winyah in Georgetown. And there is no denying that the occasion is a stylish and remarkably beautiful happening, especially as one strolls the grounds of one of the country's most elegant plantation manor houses.

In the past, what now is known as Arcadia existed as separate plantations—including Clifton, Prospect Hill, Rose Hill, Forlorn Hope, George Hill, Oak Hill, Fairfield, Bannockburn, and Debordieu Beach. Today's mansion is the one that stood at Prospect Hill Plantation.

When one approaches the house from U.S. 17, on the right of the highway between Pawley's Island and Georgetown, sometimes one will encounter a deer; stopping in the sandy lane, it looks at the approaching car as though it were an intruder, then dashes into the woods. And suddenly the visitor is out of the woods and entering the grounds through an ancient gate, and the celebrated mansion looms sky high. This house has always been considered a breath-taking sight. An avenue of moss-festooned oaks runs between the tennis courts and the house, and the stables are on the left, away from the residence. On the right side, near the house, is a huge structure that once housed an indoor pool; later it became a gym, and today it serves as a guest house.

The old gateposts near the river are engraved with these words: "Prospect Hill, Founded in 1740." Seen from the river, the graceful plantation house calls to mind the past, the life lived by the rice planters. Two rice millstones are open to view under a live oak tree. Coming closer, however, one is impressed with activities very much in the present, as people of all ages, casually dressed, come and go. The present owner of Arcadia has a large and lively family who enjoy the swimming pool, stables and tennis courts as well as the architecturally splendid house. Despite its history, this is also a house of today, with furniture upholstered in lime green, lemon-yellow, and pink; with flowered pillows embroidered in bright colors, family photographs, and youngsters with pets. "I don't want the children to grow up in a museum," says the owner. "You're as liable as not to stumble on a toy truck when you come in the door."

Prospect Hill was settled in the mid-1700s by William Alston; afterwards it came into the possession first of Joseph Alston, and then of Thomas Alston. Thomas had married a cousin, Mary Allston; they had no children. He died in 1794, and the plantation with the beautiful mansion went to his widow. In 1796 Mary

Prospect Hill Plantation manor house at Arcadia Plantation. From this entrance a carpet was laid to the boat landing prior to the visit of President James Monroe.
Photograph by SID RHYNE.

married Benjamin Huger II, a member of another prominent family of rice planters. The bride and groom toured New England after their wedding, then came home to Prospect Hill in the fall. Huger was elected to the South Carolina House of Representatives and also served in Congress, but he continued to enjoy living and entertaining at Prospect Hill. It was a solid, spacious home where business could be carried on and family life celebrated, both of which were important to the rice planters. And as the house had touches of grandeur and could boast to the world of the family's success, so much the better!

President James Monroe visited the Waccamaw region in 1819, and Benjamin Huger invited him to come to Prospect Hill. As preparations were made for the occasion, Huger wrote a welcoming address, referring to George Washington's visit to the Low Country thirty years earlier. Mrs. Huger designed and started the planting of the now-famous garden.

President Monroe arrived by boat at the canal that led from the Waccamaw River to the Prospect Hill Plantation landing. Just before the President's craft arrived, Huger placed a roll of carpet at the foot of the portico steps and unrolled it to the very spot where the President would disembark from his boat. When President Monroe stepped ashore, his feet fell upon the carpet. As he walked up the incline to the mansion, not one grain of Low-Country sand stuck to his shoes. Only by seeing the distance involved can one realize the magnitude of carpeting from the veranda to the canal, but perhaps this luxury is a fair measure of the grand manner in which the planters lived. The Reverend Dr. H.D. Bull, who once served All Saints Church as rector, wrote that President Monroe later was conveyed from Prospect Hill to Georgetown in a plantation barge which had been profusely decorated for the occasion with the United States colors proudly floating at its head. Eight black oarsmen dressed in livery propelled the barge.

After Benjamin Huger's death on July 7, 1823, his wife sold Prospect Hill to Colonel Joshua John Ward of Brookgreen; Ward in turn left the plantation to his son, Benjamin Huger Ward. Benjamin Huger Ward died in 1903, and Dr. Isaac E. Emerson of Baltimore bought the plantation from his heirs in 1906. Dr. Emerson, a chemist, had attended the University of North Carolina at Chapel Hill. After completing his education, he invented

Bromo Seltzer and made a fortune from the product. The Bromo Seltzer plant was in Baltimore, but the company which made boxes for the product was located near Georgetown, South Carolina, so Emerson came to know the area quite well.

Emerson bought several plantations and named the property Arcadia, rather than continuing to refer to each plantation by its old name. He added the north and south wings to enlarge the mansion and built a large guest house. Emerson also had the gardens cleared of overgrowth and developed them into a showplace of terraces, gateways, pools and bridges.

The Emersons had one child, Margaret, who married Alfred Gwynne Vanderbilt. Vanderbilt died in the sinking of the *Lusitania* when that passenger ship of the Cunard Line was torpedoed by a German submarine off the coast of Ireland on May 7, 1915. Although he was a poor swimmer, Vanderbilt gave his lifebelt to a woman. Of his two sons, the older one owned and raced horses, and at the age of twenty-one his mother gave him her own racing stable, Sagamore. The younger son, George, inherited Arcadia in 1936 from his grandfather.

The Man Of The House Of Vanderbilt

George Young remembers how, and even precisely when, he first began to learn the mannerisms, traits, and disposition that would take him to the top in the George Vanderbilt mansions. Annie Young, George's mother, was a cook at Arcadia. Annie's dark hands moved swift and sure, as she prepared the foods so desired by Vanderbilt and his wealthy visitors.

George recalls how his mother's rare learning and her low musical language made their way into his heart as he watched her work in the large, well-equipped kitchen. Annie's husband took care of the Vanderbilt horses and dogs, a strenuous task. But George portrays the quiet ease of his mother as he speaks of her poise and the lightness of her footfalls as she came and went from the Vanderbilt kitchen.

As a child, George began to perceive that he could be like his mother and could even learn to cook like her. She would be his model and perhaps someday he, too, could cook in that kitchen.

One day Mr. Vanderbilt asked George if he would set up the tables for a dinner after a deer hunt at Debordieu, Vanderbilt's seashore portion of his estate. George considered the request a great honor. He knew what to do. He had watched, and he had remembered.

"Mr. Vanderbilt never allowed drinks to be served until after the dinner which followed the deer hunt," George recounted. All the while that George was getting the tables ready for the dinner, he was watching the man who was barbecuing meat.

"He didn't know I was watching him, but I wanted to learn how to cook meat by barbecuing it just like I'd learned to cook by watching my mother. Every now and then, when they'd killed a deer, they would bring a quarter of the meat to the barbecue pit. The cook would baste the meat with barbecue sauce and cook the deer meat on the grill. A well was nearby. This place was near the ocean but not too close. It was back in the trees.

"My father had set up the stands for the hunters. There were four or five stands, in different places, far apart so there was no danger of anyone getting shot."

"Who were some of Mr. Vanderbilt's guests?" George was asked.

He laughed in hearty mirth. "Oh, there were so many wealthy and famous people. I remember Miss Ginger Rogers, and Peter Duchin. And sometimes Alan Ladd and John Wayne were here. Oh, they loved to come to Arcadia Plantation."

"Did they always hunt deer?"

"Oh, no. They went duck shooting a lot of the time." Just at that moment George was suddenly convulsed in a gale of laughter. "Mr. Vanderbilt kept a list of the kinds of ducks they were likely to shoot," he said. "Let me see—on the list was mallard, teal, pintail and others. But at the bottom of the list was 'brown rabbit.' Mr. Vanderbilt always checked the list and told how many ducks, and the kinds of ducks, that were killed that day. But if someone fell overboard he would check 'brown rabbit.' The guests didn't know what that meant. They thought it was a kind of duck. And almost every time they went hunting for ducks someone would fall overboard. You know, they'd be standing in the boat, and when they pulled the trigger, the gun would jar them, and over they went. At night, usually at dinner, Mr. Vanderbilt would take his list and call out the number of ducks killed that day. And he'd call out to me and say, 'George we got two brown rabbits this afternoon.' I knew that meant that two people had fallen overboard. And the water was cold."

"How did Mr. Vanderbilt handle it when someone fell overboard?"

"He had towels and blankets in the boat, always."

George explained that Mr. Vanderbilt didn't like to hunt ducks too much. "But he always had guides and the boats were always ready to be taken. One time Mr. Vanderbilt told me that he was expecting a very special guest. I was getting bigger by that time and some of the work was assigned to me when guests were expected. On this occasion a Prince from Europe was coming to hunt ducks. And do you know what? That Prince fell overboard.

And the boat was brought back to the plantation house immediately so the Prince could be warmed up. The guide was Snowey, and Snowey came flying in with the Prince and everybody got all excited."

"What did Mr. Vanderbilt think about that?"

"He laughed, and that's the God's truth. He said, 'George, we got a brown rabbit today.' "

George Vanderbilt had many boats for the use of his visitors. They had names like *The Adroit, The Alligator,* and *The Arcadia.* Most of the visitors arrived in Georgetown by yacht, and one of the Vanderbilt boats would be there to bring them to the plantation via the Waccamaw River.

George Young was adept and learned almost every facet of running the plantation. "When I first started working in the house, I was bringing in wood, scrubbing the floor and washing dishes," he said. "Finally I learned to do about everything the other household help did. Mr. Vanderbilt employed people from France, Germany, Italy, Sweden and Hawaii. And he had three butlers. I worked under all of them and learned their tricks of the trade. Sometime later, the three butlers had a misunderstanding. I don't know what happened, but Mr. Vanderbilt didn't like that. He called me upstairs and said, 'George, I can't stand this. The butlers are fighting and arguing all the time. I can't have it. You must learn how to run this house because I'm going to get rid of them and give the whole job to you!"

George pointed out that he had had no schooling for being a butler or running such a magnificent, huge house. "Those butlers all went to school to learn how to do their work," George explained. He believed that he lacked both knowledge of the traditions Mr. Vanderbilt would want upheld and the efficient management skills he would need. After all, a good butler was a status symbol, like a Rolls Royce. George Young wondered if he could become an ideal butler, a model of understated competence.

"I tell you, George, I think you can do it," Vanderbilt said.

"I'll try," George promised.

Within a few weeks, Vanderbilt fired his three butlers and told George Young to take over the mansion. Twenty-five people would report to him. Everything progressed wonderfully and Mr. Vanderbilt was pleased with the work of George Young, the man who had been born on the plantation and attended the little plantation schoolhouse. It was plain to see that George Young had learned how to run a mansion.

"One night Mr. Vanderbilt came in from the beach and asked me to meet him upstairs," George Young recalls.

"Sit down, George, I want to talk to you," Vanderbilt said.

"Boss, I don't have time to sit down. I have to go back downstairs and get everything ready for dinner tonight."

"George Young! You have four or five people down there who are supposed to know how to get dinner ready."

"Well they can do it, but I need to be there too, to see that everything is done according to my wishes," George explained.

"I know that," Vanderbilt said. "You try to do it all. You're the one who does all the work around here."

"Well, boss, I just want to see that it's done right"

"Don't you have a second man?" Vanderbilt asked.

"Yes. But I want to be around too."

"George, you have all those people working for you and I've never known you to have the slightest argument with a single one of them. You are the best I've ever had at running a big house." Vanderbilt explained that he wanted to have this expert supervision in all of his houses. He wanted George to travel with him and visit his other homes.

George Young was to travel with George Vanderbilt to his homes in Palm Beach and New York City, his ranch in California, and his house in Hawaii. But they always returned to Arcadia.

"Arcadia was his favorite place," George commented. "He loved it here. One night when we were here he told me to get ready to go to San Francisco, and from there to Hawaii.

"Boss, I said, 'I want to build a house.'

"You want to build a house?'

"Yes."

Vanderbilt talked George into accompanying him on the trip. One day while they were away Vanderbilt handed George a letter. "Do you have any girlfriends?" he asked.

George Young ripped open the envelope. To his surprise, it

contained the deed and accompanying papers to five acres of land adjoining Arcadia Plantation. Vanderbilt had deeded the land to George Young; later he would help him build a house there.

Today George Young runs a barbecue business on his property. He has a bad hip and the arthritis in his knees is a nuisance, but he cooks in the same manner as he cooked at the house of Vanderbilt. Customer after customer stop at the barbecue establishment for ribs, chicken and chopped barbecue. If they're lucky, some is available for sale. Mostly, George Young's barbecued meat is catered to parties, receptions and pig-pickings held at Grand Strand hotels.

"I guess I'll keep on working here until they have to take me out," Young said, testing a panorama of pork shoulders he was smoking in a sheet metal outdoor cooker. The aroma of the cooking meat was tantalizing. The cook would only turn away from the cooker to sum up his feelings about the late George Vanderbilt.

"I tell you, Missy, I miss him like I miss my mother."

Miss Belle Baruch.
Photograph by Miss Ella Severin.

For Whom This Belle Tolls

Almost every person dreams of a special place to own if there were no financial limitations. In 1905 Bernard Baruch, after amassing a fortune on Wall Street, purchased just such a place—Hobcaw Barony, the southernmost third of the Waccamaw peninsula, which juts into Winyah Bay. He transformed the area into a place where fact is more exciting than fiction. (This property is on the left of U.S. 17 as you travel from Pawley's Island to Georgetown, and a portion of it is on the opposite side of the highway from Arcadia.) You can visit Hobcaw for a tour, but it's best to call first, as the tours are conducted in vans which can accommodate only small groups.

In 1718 one of Carolina's largest land tracts was first granted to John, Lord Carteret, one of the Lords Proprietors. Through the years, parcels of the original grant were sold as separate plantations, bequeathed, and otherwise changed hands many times. As each generation of planters died off and their executors divided their estates according to their wills, it was inevitable that large acreages would be divided and subdivided. The thirteen separate rice plantations were divided by a series of boundary ditches, which created mounds on each side. The ditches served as boundary lines, and the mounds are in evidence today. Baruch had the resources to trace the titles to lands contained in the original barony and purchase everything except for three plantations at the northern end of the tract. His acquisition actually extended beyond the original barony and amounted to some 17,500 acres. For him it was a return to a special place which he had visited. He remembered the mild climate, the sea, the salt marshes, the ancient forests, the rice fields, and the wildlife. Especially the wildlife. Baruch once said that he had hunted in Canada, Czechoslovakia and Scotland, but none compared with coastal South Carolina in variety and abundance of game.

The Baruchs, who lived in New York, spent winters at Friendfield Plantation, usually coming at Thanksgiving and leaving at the end of April. Friendfield House was not elaborate, but the Baruch children called it "quaint and old-fashioned," unlike the apartments they were accustomed to in New York City. The Baruch children were Belle, Renee and Bernard Jr.

At the time the Baruchs first came to Hobcaw, a large number of people who had been born in slavery and their descendants were living on the property. Baruch said that they expected him to provide them with work. In an effort to make jobs, he tried to produce rice, but the venture failed. Some of the people left the plantation to seek employment elsewhere. For the old and disabled, Baruch set up a system whereby they could obtain groceries in Georgetown and pay when they had funds. He called his credit arrangement an "old-age pension plan."

The Baruchs and their guests, including Key Pittman, a U. S. senator, were at Friendfield House during the Christmas holidays in 1929 when they were surprised by a fire spreading through the attic. Some furniture was saved, as well as a "barrel of good corn likker," but the Baruchs and their guest stood on the front lawn and watched as the house was engulfed and destroyed by flames.

A new mansion was built on the bluff overlooking Winyah Bay. The new dwelling was constructed of brick, steel and concrete to make it as fireproof as possible. Although the house style is the Colonial Revival style so popular in the 1930s, it resembles the antebellum plantation style. Beyond the massive oaks draped in moss is the bay where Baruch's boats, *Eagle Point, Sea Dog* and *The Chick*, rode at anchor.

Although the house had central heating, each of the ten bedrooms had a fireplace and adjoining bath. Mrs. Raoul Fleischmann of New York, who later became an owner of *The New Yorker*, decorated the home.

At the northern boundary of the garden, Baruch had a playhouse built for his daughters. The structure was as large as some of the old buildings on the plantation. Inside were a stove and sink, and the children baked cookies for Christmas parties traditionally held in their playhouse.

Many noted people visited the Baruchs, and there is a photograph in a bedroom inscribed, "For Belle, with affection and friendship. Edith Bolling Wilson, July 10, 1924." When Sir Winston Churchill and his daughter Diana came to Hobcaw in 1932, Diana said that she simply *must* find a horse to ride, a request that posed no problem because Baruch maintained a well-stocked stable. Baruch's relationship with Churchill was close, and they exchanged over 700 letters.

But few of Baruch's associations were as richly satisfying as his friendship with Franklin D. Roosevelt. On Easter Sunday in 1944, when World War II was flaming in Europe, a car pulled up to the Hobcaw gate. A passenger, in a Navy cape that was drawn over his face, was waved on. When the car stopped under the oaks in front of the mansion and the passenger emerged, a small boy standing back in the shadows said, "Gosh. It's George Washington!" The visitor was not George Washington, of course, but President Roosevelt.

For reasons of security, Roosevelt traveled in strictest secrecy when he came to Hobcaw and, as a precaution against assassination, soldiers from Fort Jackson were stationed throughout the miles and miles of forests. They were clothed in uniforms dyed green with leaves painted on them. Pine needles and oak leaves were attached to their helmets, hands and feet. The soldiers in their camouflaged uniforms so blended into the forests that Belle Baruch said, "If another tree moves, I'll scream!"

Belle W. Baruch purchased for a cash amount the entire property known as Hobcaw Barony, and she had a house built for herself to complement the contour and atmosphere of the wildlife area she loved so well. A sitting room had a lofty ceiling with exposed wood beams, adorned by stuffed animals and deer antlers. A stuffed bobcat crouched on the hearth, an extremely *real* looking bobcat. Portraits of horses crowded the walls—notable among them a picture of Belle riding her favorite horse, Souriant, painted by a well-known artist of that day, Alfred J. Munnings.

Belle was a pilot, and kept her plane at Hobcaw. She flew low, just over the treetops and screamed, "Look at the deer!" She was also a trophy-winning yachtsman. But her passion was horses. She rode and trained horses near her home, Bellefield, and showed them all over the world. In 1931 she received the La Coupe du President (French President's Cup) as the winner of the classic competition in the Paris horse show. In the 1931 contest she was the only one of 119 contestants, including French cavalry officers, to make a perfect score. By that time she had already won more than 300 prizes in France and other countries, and was maintaining a large stable at Pau, France.

It was Belle who probably made the most important decision ever to be made about Hobcaw Barony—to change the land from a hunting and fishing preserve to a research laboratory for the study of forests and marine estuaries. She couldn't bear to think of the historical area being overrun by careless tourists when she would no longer be there to protect it.

Belle Baruch felt that nowhere else in the United States existed that particular combination of forest, marshlands, beaches and canals that curved and tracked to the sea, and she felt a unique responsibility to work out a plan for the use of forest and marshes in research programs. When her will was drawn, she set up a foundation to implement her plan.

On Saturday, April 25, 1964 Belle Baruch died. She was sixty-four. On June 20, 1965 Bernard Baruch died of a heart attack at his apartment in New York City. He was ninety-four.

Under the terms of Belle's will, Clemson University assumed responsibility for conducting research and teaching forestry and wildlife management science, and the University of South Carolina became responsible for research and teaching in marine and coastal areas. Sinuous ribbons of salt-tolerant grasses, reeds and rushes capable of enduring exposure to the sun and drying winds are among the major research subjects of the University of South Carolina. The amount of nutrients produced by the fast-growing marsh grass at Hobcaw is almost unbelievable.

The forest at Hobcaw provides Clemson University a valuable laboratory for the collection of data on forest productivity. Among the unusual species of trees found are camphor, tea olive and toothache trees. Forestry research also includes testing the virgin pine trees believed to be more than one hundred fifty years old.

There is also research on the red-cockaded woodpecker—the only woodpecker in North America that builds its nests in living pines instead of dead ones. The red-cockaded woodpeckers' chances for survival are jeopardized as their nesting trees are being logged in other parts of the country. But the plight of the tiny black and white woodpecker is receiving serious attention at Hobcaw. It is estimated that between seventy-five and one hundred red-cockaded woodpeckers live on the plantation, and their habits are being studied.

Other funds have been added to the investment held by the Belle Baruch Foundation. The National Science Foundation included the North Inlet Estuary in its five-year Long Term Ecological Research Program as the estuarine site for the U. S., and the program has been renewed for another five years.

In the forest at Hobcaw, there are herds of deer, wild turkeys and quail, and ducks that still winter on plantation waters. But instead of a hunter raising the viewfinder of a gun, one sees a scientist looking through a telescope as he zeroes in on a subject. And in the marsh, if a man leans over the side of a boat with a

Hobcaw House where Bernard Baruch was host to notables such as Sir Winston Churchill and Franklin D. Roosevelt.
Photograph by SID RHYNE.

container, he isn't lifting seafood for the table but a sample of water to be tested under a microscope.

The house of white clapboard and rosy brick at Bellefield stands in the shade of oaks, and higher-than-your-head azaleas blaze red and pink in April—the prettiest month, according to Bernard Baruch. The house, occupied by a working trustee of the Belle Baruch Foundation, is not open to the public. Miss Ella A. Severin, a lady born in Sweden but one who is perfectly suited to the task of perpetuating Bellefield House in the tradition of Belle Baruch, lives at Bellefield today. She is committed to the fulfillment of Belle's wishes, and as a trustee of the Foundation she oversees the progress and work of the trustees.

Bellefield House has many reminders of "way back when." A framed memento on a wall is the notice in a Charleston newspaper of a runaway slave. The notice appeared under the usual woodcut imprint of a head of a slave. Souriant is buried near the stable and the gravesite is surrounded by a white fence. In the stable are hundreds of trophies of every size and shape won by Belle when showing her horses.

Because of the area's still low level of industrialization, the waters around Hobcaw Barony are miraculously unpolluted, and many people in the area eat some form of fish at every meal. Furthermore, because of the proximity of the water to the Low-Country mania for freshness, fish is almost certain to have been caught within the past twenty-four hours.

But for the farsightedness of Belle Baruch, this virgin land could be gleaming in the sun with white high-rise condominiums, bronzed bodies relaxing by pools, and golfers sending little white balls zinging down fairways. Instead, Hobcaw Barony will always be a natural habitat for Low-Country growth and animals. And for the flora and fauna, and the people in research, at Hobcaw this Belle still tolls.

The Signer In The Sea

From the impressive ruins of Peachtree Plantation on the South Santee River one can see Hopsewee Plantation, across the delta on the other split of the river, the North Santee River. Hopsewee, 16 miles south of Georgetown, indicates a place that figures in the nation's earliest history as the home of Thomas Lynch, a delegate to the first Continental Congress, and Thomas Lynch Jr., a signer of the Declaration of Independence. The word Hopsewee is believed to have been derived from Hop, the name of a Cherokee Indian chief, and the Sewee Indians who lived on the coast near the Santee River.

Hopsewee House, built by Thomas Lynch Sr. about 1737, was constructed of black cypress. Its foundations were of brick covered by scored tabby, a mixture of sand, lime and oyster shells introduced by the Spaniards. Tabby construction was common in the area when there was a large labor force to do the manual labor. Shells were there for the taking, and lime was made in kilns built by the slaves. Although some fortresses and churches were built of tabby, especially in the Beaufort area, in this region it was used mostly for foundations. It has been said that the best recipe for tabby is to mix two buckets of gravel, one of lime and four of oyster shells. (Cement had not been perfected in the Colonial era.)

Hopsewee House is open to the public. Entering the porch on the river side, as guests usually do, one comes into a hallway that runs through the center of the house. On the right is the drawing room. Here one sees the lovely candlelight mouldings and mantel, hand-carved in the pattern made famous by the Adam brothers of Scotland. Looking down, one sees the original floors, made of pine boards one and one-half inches thick. Crossing the hallway, one enters the dining room, where again the attention is caught by the candlelight moulding. Here the chair rails form deep window sills. Doors are hung with H and L hinges, and close attention reveals that the panels are raised on one side but recessed on the other.

The room that is used today as a family kitchen has a hint of the West Indies that blends with its Colonial design. Near the brick fireplace is a hook that, many years ago, held a rope that was attached to a turkey tail fan. The little fly-brush boy tugged the rope to wave the fan over the table and shoo away flies. During the prime of this plantation, the kitchen was in an outside building which still stands. The architecture of that building also has a West Indies influence.

The candlelight moulding runs upstairs and through the center hallway, where a framed document on the wall reminds the visitor that Thomas Lynch Jr. was born in this house in August 1749. Lynch had a tragic life, despite his wealth and social position. He was educated at Eton and the University of Cambridge and studied law at the Inns of Court in London. By the time he returned to South Carolina in 1772, his father had sold Hopsewee and built a new house at Peachtree Plantation, across the river.

In the family tradition, young Lynch plunged into Revolutionary politics and service to his state, even though he was in poor health. His father had always accepted political duties and posts when asked and was elected to every Assembly, except one, from 1751 until the Revolution; he was also the first president of the Winyah Indigo Society in Georgetown. The Santee planters were considered to be residents of the parish of St. James Santee, although in a census they were listed as growing rice in the Georgetown District. At the first meeting of the Provincial Congress in January 1775, Thomas Lynch Sr. represented Prince George Winyah and Thomas Lynch Jr. represented St. James Santee.

When the time came to appoint a delegation to represent the state in the Second Continental Congress, the provincial congress chose Thomas Lynch Jr. as a delegate to assist his father, who had become feeble in mind and body. The Declaration of Independence was adopted and released to the public on July 4, 1776. Lynch Sr. was too ill to sign, but Lynch Jr. signed with the rest of the South Carolina delegation. He was twenty-six.

Some months later, as the Lynches were making their way back to South Carolina, Thomas Lynch Sr. died in Maryland and was buried at Annapolis. Thomas Lynch Jr. came on home and he lived with his wife, the former Elizabeth Shubrick, at Peachtree Plantation. From the river entrance to their home they could view Hopsewee, which Thomas Lynch Sr. had sold to Robert Hume.

Thomas Lynch Jr. lost his vigor and well-being, and as disease overtook his body he searched his mind for any manner of restoration. As he sat in a chair, his face pallid and his body actually shaking from anguish and agony, he uttered a word of command. His wife was to make plans for them to sail to the West Indies and then continue to the south of France, where Lynch hoped he would regain his strength. Elizabeth Lynch was aware of the risk of traveling on the seas at that time: storms which came quickly, without warning, and pirates who operated off the coast of South Carolina and preyed on ships under all flags.

But Elizabeth Lynch swiftly made travel plans, and she and Thomas sailed toward the West Indies. The ship on which Thomas and Elizabeth Lynch sailed was lost at sea. The young signer of the Declaration of Independence was only thirty when he died.

The old kitchen at Hopsewee Plantation. Note the West Indian influence in the architecture of this shingled building.
Photograph by SID RHYNE.

The steps are all that is left of The Elms Plantation.
Photograph by SID RHYNE.

The Glory Of The Izards And The Elms

Millions of Americans have had a glimpse of the Low Country's plantation past, a look at her vast and imposing landscapes, a taste of her sensuality and complexity. But the age of peacocks, palaces and Charleston balls is long past. A very contemporary generation is at the helm of what was once The Elms, the country seat of the Izard family. The fabulous mansion was destroyed in the earthquake of 1886, and although the house and family are gone, the magic spell lingers.

The Goose Creek section, seventeen miles from Charleston near the Cooper River, was a very protected little world when the first Ralph Izard arrived in South Carolina in 1682. But like those who would follow him in the Izard family, Ralph was industrious and obtained grants to large tracts of land, some in Goose Creek and some in Wassamassaw. In 1686 he married the widow of Arthur Middleton and through this "good marriage" obtained even more land.

As one who delighted in fulfilling the expectations of others, after the first Ralph Izard had acquired a fortune, he held political office in the provincial government. His son Ralph was appointed to the Grand Council of the Lords Proprietors in 1719. His fashionable home on Goose Creek was named The Elms, and at his death it passed to Henry Izard, who at his death left it to his son, another Ralph Izard.

That Ralph Izard had an extraordinary zest for life. At the age of twelve he was enrolled in the Hackney School in England, and he finished his education at Cambridge. On May 1, 1767 he returned to South Carolina and promptly married Miss Alice DeLancey of Westchester, New York. In 1769 Ralph and Alice visited Europe; while there, they chose to spend their summers in

London and their winters in Rome. In Rome they sat for the noted portrait by Copley which hangs in the Museum of Fine Arts in Boston. Finally, they returned to South Carolina.

Ralph Izard and Pierce Butler were the first U. S. senators to represent South Carolina in Congress. Izard served from 1789 to 1795 and was President Pro Tem of the Senate.

When the house at The Elms burned in 1809, Ralph and Alice replaced it with a beautiful mansion. Their desire was that their new manor house be prominent as a center of the social life of the Goose Creek region.

On the creek side of the house, the recessed portico roof was supported by heavy columns. Entering the mansion from that side, one came into a square hall with staircase. On each side of the hall was an octagonal room. From the porticoed entrance on the inland side one entered the hall, and on each side was a huge rectangular room.

The mansion, constructed on a bluff on the 4,350-acre plantation was surrounded by formal gardens. Outbuildings consisted of a gazebo and carriage house; there was a boat landing and, of course, a well-stocked wine cellar. The family arms were embossed in plaster on various parts of the exterior edifice. Besides The Elms, the Izards owned five other rice-producing plantations. After Ralph Izard retired from public life, he and Alice lived quietly at The Elms.

The house passed out of the Izard family in 1826 when it was sold to settle the estate of Ralph's son Henry. It continued to stand in fair condition until a major earthquake rumbled through the Charleston area in 1886.

The earthquake of August 31, 1886 was preceded by light tremors. The great shock came at 9:51 p.m. The area disturbed encompassed 2,800,000 square miles, the largest on record. Buildings near the epicenter which were not completely demolished were wrecked. Property damage exceeded five million dollars and ninety-two people lost their lives.

The Elms and the Izards were synonymous of the glory of a long ago time, but no trace of their splendor remains. From 1906 the property was part of the Goose Creek watershed. It was sold to The Baptist College of Lower South Carolina.

Boone Hall Plantation Portrayed Mont Royal in *North and South*

Boone Hall Plantation, adjacent to U.S. 17 north of Charleston's Cooper River Bridge, was built by members of the South Carolina aristocracy. Although it is located in Christ Church Parish, it is so striking in beauty and rich in the history of the South that it was the perfect setting to serve as Mont Royal Plantation, which John Jakes placed in Saint George's Parish in his novels. Mont Royal Plantation was the home of Orry Main in David L. Wolper's production of *North and South,* an epic ABC miniseries based on Jakes' bestselling novels.

Among the props left at Boone Hall after the filming was completed are the white grape arbors between the black iron gates and the mansion, the split rail fence enclosed vegetable garden, a hitching post and the burial place of Orry's father, near two huge oak trees. An oak tree near the fake vegetable garden is over 250 years old.

Boone Hall was a rice plantation, but not in the sense of some other, more productive rice plantations. The Boones consumed most of the rice they raised. Later on, this plantation on Wampacheone Creek became important in the output of cotton. The cotton gin, where the fiber was separated from the seed, can be seen today, as well as the creek landing where the barges were loaded with bales of cotton. Wampacheone Creek works its way to the ocean.

Unlike most Old South plantations, Boone Hall is still a working plantation. For a fee, it is open to the public, and visitors can plainly see that it is a living link between the country's past and present. The owners are the inheritors and conservators of a cherished way of life.

As you drive through the three-quarter mile avenue of moss-draped live oaks, do not assume that this is the property of a duke, a marquess or an earl, although Boone Hall Plantation has many of the same embellishments as a nobleman's house. This beautiful avenue dates back to 1743 and is famous the world over. The facade of the mansion was the inspiration for Twelve Oaks, the Wilkes family seat.

Visitors park and then wait on the piazza until the next tour of the house begins. Young ladies in Colonial finery escort visitors through the mansion. Their dialogue beings in the library/music room.

"This plantation was named after Major John Boone, who was among the first group of English settlers to come to South Caro-

Among the props left at Boone Hall Plantation after the filming of NORTH AND SOUTH was completed are the white grape arbors. Boone Hall portrayed Mont Royal Plantation in David L. Wolper's production of the two epic ABC miniseries based on John Jakes' novels.
Photograph by SID RHYNE.

lina. In 1618 he received a land grant from the Lords Proprietors of England for seventeen thousand acres of land. The Boones were a Christian family and were among the few planters to educate their slaves. The slaves were schooled in the commissary with the Boone children.

"The Boones left in 1806; they moved to China to establish a missionary colony. In 1817 Major John S. Holbeck bought the plantation and cultivated the pecan groves that were the largest in the world at that time. In 1935 Thomas Stone bought the plantation and made major renovations of the house turning it into an antebellum mansion by adding the white-columned piazza. In 1954 the McRae family, who are the present owners of the plantation, bought the property. They were from Ellerbe, North Carolina.

"Today the plantation on Wampacheone Creek covers 738 acres. Cattle and vegetables are grown here. Boone Hall is one of the few working plantations in the country.

"This library/music room is where the ladies would go for their recreation time. The floor is made of random-sized oak boards taken from old Charleston homes that were demolished. If you look closely, you will see that the boards are put together with wooden pegs. The walls are cypress and have hand-carved decoration at the top. To the right of the fireplace is a tilt-top table that dates from 1780. The picture over the fireplace is called 'Queen of the May.' It was done in 1841 and depicts a celebration. The coffee table, made of mahogany, dates from the 1850s. The couch and two matching chairs are from Rome, Italy. They date from 1840 and were constructed of olive wood. The piano is a Knabe original, made in Baltimore, and is over a hundred and twenty years old. It's still in good working order, with the original keys and strings."

Passing from that room to the entrance hall, the visitors are reminded that the library/music room was used as Orry Main's office in the Jakes films.

"The free-flying staircase here in the entrance hall has no visible means of support, except at the top and bottom. Under the staircase stands a grandmother clock. It has three sets of chimes. To be a grandfather clock, it would have to be six feet, six inches tall. This one is six feet. The hall bench is the oldest piece of furniture in the house. It's a McRae family heirloom. It dates from 1560. In those days, the artists didn't carve their signatures into the work; instead they carved images of themselves."

There are two busts on the top of the bench, one at each end. The faces are pleasant. Both men are wearing hats and their hair is shoulder-length. One face is clean-shaven, while the other has a mustache and goatee. There is a faint sense of mirth radiating from the tiny faces.

"Also, here is a petticoat table with a low mirror, so that the ladies could check their wide skirts and make sure a petticoat wasn't evident. In that day it was perfectly disgraceful for an ankle to show, much less a petticoat."

The hostess calls attention to the front door, which is called a "Christian door" because of the cross carved in the African mahogany.

Entering the dining room, visitors might be struck with the thought that to open a stately home and unfurl the treasures requires more entertainer-like flair than squirearchal solidity. Especially in the dining room you are aware of the drama of the planter families as the hostess parades the valuables.

"The mahogany-framed mirror is eleven feet tall, and it rests on a mahogany base. The mirror was placed here to give an illusion of the room being much larger, and also to reflect light. In the corner is a china cabinet that was hand-carved in the mid-1800s. The glass panes are beveled. 'Welcome' is represented by the carved torches on the top, while the carved ropes on the sides represent wealth. Within is a porcelain service that was dipped in twenty-two carat gold, and the coffee service is cobalt blue, dipped in twenty-four carat gold. Prince Albert is the design. The service in the cabinet on the opposite side of the room is also cobalt blue and twenty-four carat gold. The Crown Derby design service is a hundred and twenty-five years old, and it's a complete setting for sixteen people. No pieces are missing, broken or chipped. The hunt board at the back of the room was used to serve the men a buffet-style breakfast before the morning hunt. The serpentine Hepplewhite buffet of rosewood dates from 1790, and the mahogany table is Queen Anne. Dining chairs of the same wood are in the Chippendale style, and the chandelier of brass and crystal was originally operated by gas. It dates from 1840."

To this day, in spite of the South's seemingly radical changes, the pull toward land remains. New money continues to buy estates, and the families model themselves after the old gentry.

They take up fox hunting, or shooting—or polo, as is the custom at Boone Hall. When the film crews arrived at Boone Hall Plantation, they discovered that it was the perfect place to portray the Main family seat, although some of the interior scenes were filmed in Charleston with its fabulous houses and banquet-sized rooms (such as the Calhoun mansion on Meeting Street, which represented the Hazard home in Pennsylvania).

Whether it's the McRaes or the Mains, Boone Hall or Mont Royal, it's a landed family and a magnificent, impressive estate.

Some of the scenes in NORTH AND SOUTH were filmed in Charleston, with its fabulous old houses and banquet-sized rooms. The Calhoun Mansion on Meeting Street portrayed the Hazard home in Pennsylvania.
Photograph by SID RHYNE.

Drayton Hall on the Ashley River is reflected in a front lawn pool.
Photograph by SID RHYNE.

The Girl Who Stopped An Army

Sherman was on the march, and the owners of the palatial mansions by the Ashley River were frightened beyond belief. Their homes were among the finest in the land, and if the enemy arrived, those homes would be burned to ashes.

Quite suddenly, a company of Yankee sympathizers formed on Johns Island and took as its goal the burning of every mansion on the Ashley.

Dr. Drayton, the owner of the most extraordinary mansion facing the Ashley, couldn't bear the thought of losing the house that had been in his family for generations. In an effort to thwart the company of intruders, he called on a brave dark-skinned girl who was working as a nurse in his house, helping him treat victims of smallpox. Dr. Drayton came up with a scheme that just might work if the girl were brave enough to carry it out. If she could, then Drayton Hall—the first great home in America to be built in the Palladian villa style of architecture—would be saved for future generations.

U.S. 61 is a busy thoroughfare until it nears Drayton Hall, and then it becomes more like an old-time road; it is so pleasant and serene, that when one first lays eyes on the house, its magnitude and grandeur are startling.

Seven generations of Draytons grew up here after John Drayton moved his family into the mansion he built between 1738 and 1742. He desired to build a splendid house, one that would be known throughout the land for its grace and beauty. John had been born at Magnolia (today known as Magnolia Gardens), which adjoined his property. But he was not the eldest son and would never inherit Magnolia. As a result, he endeavored to build a mansion that would surpass the magnificence of his birthplace.

Those who visit Drayton Hall today see many reminders of the Drayton families who lived there, even though all furniture is gone. On the doorframe of an upstairs bedroom closet are the height measurements of Drayton children, and there is also the height measurement of a dog named Ripper. (A Drayton descendant explains that the animal supported itself on its hind legs to attain the marked height.)

Walls of bald cypress are decorated with carvings in the form of chains of foliage, fruit and flowers. The light and shadows from candles must have glimmered on the beautifully cast plaster ceilings. (There is no electricity or plumbing in the mansion today.) The windows have deep window seats and shutters which protected against the high winds of hurricanes.

Wainscoting in the principal rooms extends from floor to ceiling, and over the large mantels are frames in the wainscoting for pictures of coats of arms. The dogwood motif appears on some of the moulding and other woodwork, as well as flowers much like sunflowers. A boar's head has been carved within the broken pediment over the mantel in the great hall at the front of the house. Look carefully, and you will see a tiny seashell in the teeth of the boar. It is obvious that John desired his great hall to be unsurpassed in beauty and grandiosity. The pilasters, in their carved detail, are a wonder to behold.

The stairhall on the river side has been referred to as "the finest in America," and one's imagination can create a two-stories-high Christmas tree within the curve of the stairs. Some of the spindles from the staircase were used for firewood during Reconstruction, but they have been replaced.

Although the mansion was usually entered from the river side during the Colonial era, the entrance approached from U.S. 61 is the most eye-catching. A pedimented Palladian portico, with Doric and Ionic columns of Portland stone imported from England, commands attention.

This brick plantation manor house is said to have cost Drayton $90,000 in 1742, and at a glance one can see that it was a very worldly house for its time. Glittering entertainments were held in the ballroom. (There is a tiny, hidden circular stairway, and servants carried food up the stairs to the dining room, or on up another floor to the ballroom, from a basement pantry.)

In her letters, Eliza Lucas wrote of having attended balls at Drayton Hall. Eliza had come to the Province of Carolina with her father, a British officer serving in Antigua, a British possession in the West Indies. Her father had inherited extensive lands between the Stono and Ashley rivers, and he built a sturdy house of tabby there, with fourteen-inch walls. Eliza became a popular member of the Ashley River group, including the Draytons. It has been said that she first saw Colonel Charles Pinckney, her future husband, at a Drayton Hall ball.

During the Civil War Dr. John Drayton, who owned Drayton Hall, was treating some slaves who had become ill with smallpox. He moved them into his house and set up a kind of hospital, and the dark-skinned girl volunteered to help.

When the militia was nearing Drayton Hall and the owner feared destruction by fire, he called the young nurse in and handed her two yellow flags. "Post one yellow flag at the river landing," he told her, "and the other at the plantation gate." Perhaps, he reasoned, when the company of men saw the yellow flags they would leave the house.

The bold young nurse walked out of the mansion, down the steps and to the river, where she posted a yellow flag. Then she made her way through the avenue of oaks to the plantation gate. A white kerchief over her hair made a stark contrast with her dark complexion.

As she stood at the gate, holding the flag, she heard the company of men approaching. "They were slamming and banging," she was to say later. Pulling up her shoulders and straightening her back, she faced the rioters.

"This be a bootiful place," she told them, pointing to the mansion. "But it not be filled with diamonds and pearls as you're a-thinkin. It be filled with the fevers of smallpox. And iffen you come any closer, *you* be filled with the fevers of smallpox!"

The Yankee sympathizers were well aware of the dangers of the disease. The symptoms included chills, headache, backache, nausea and fever. Red spots appeared on the skin about three or four days after the disease began, and if the patient lived through it, the scabs dropped off and left pockmarks. There was no cure for smallpox, although two physicians finally resorted to an old remedy of injecting blood from recovered smallpox victims into the bodies of other persons. But most patients were afraid to take that risk.

Taking in carefully every word that the nurse had said, the soldiers eyed the mansion in the distance. Then they broke into a run, and that was the last time they were seen in the Ashley River region.

Drayton Hall is the only original mansion still standing on the Ashley River. It is now jointly owned by the National Trust and the state of South Carolina, and is operated in cooperation with the Historic Charleston Foundation.

Mepkin Plantation

After Clare Boothe Brokaw married Henry R. Luce in 1936, Bernard Baruch suggested they buy a coastal South Carolina plantation. They followed his advice, choosing Mepkin Plantation near the town of Moncks Corner. Mr. and Mrs. Nicholas G. Rutgers of Remson, New Jersey, sold the property for an estimated $150,000. Never would the Luces have imagined at the time of purchase their final use for the plantation.

According to Washington columnist Betty Beale, Clare Boothe Luce was the most brilliant, most multitalented, and wittiest of all her women friends.

There is no doubt that Clare's wit was one of her main drawing powers. Among her noted terse observations were, "No good deed goes unpunished" and "Money doesn't bring happiness, but it's a pleasant way to be miserable." It's also believed that she is responsible for another familiar quip. According to the story, Dorothy Parker once opened a door, allowing Clare to enter first. Clare swept by, saying, "Pearls before swine."

The house that had served as home to Henry Laurens (president of the first and second councils of safety, 1775–76; president of the first provincial congress of S. C., 1775; vice president of S. C., 1776; president of the Continental Congress, 1777–78; among other offices held) had been destroyed long before the Luces obtained the property, and the house that had been constructed on the old site in 1905 was not to their liking. The Luces decided they would build a home more in line with their tastes.

The modernistic house that was constructed was unlike any

other in the area. Some say it resembled a roadside motel. The structure was so unlike the treasured old plantation mansions and the famed Charleston homes, with their tall windows heavily curtained in thick velvet, it troubled the natives. The Luces' modern house was tagged with a reputation and their lifestyle looked upon with suspicion by Charleston aristocrats.

Paying no heed to public opinion, Clare hired architect Edward Durrell Stone to design four guest houses in the likeness of the main house: "functional structures of chromium and glass that glitter among the ancient trees." She named them Claremont, Tartleberry, Strawberry and Washington.

During the next six years the Luces enjoyed their plantation, giving parties, inviting friends to hunting soirees, and passing days in a dreamy haze of glorious laughter and animated talk, not all of which Clare's friends agreed with.

Finally, it occurred to Clare that her gift for strong opinion might be best suited to another stage, and in 1942 she was elected Connecticut's first congresswoman. Establishing herself as a foe of the New Deal wasn't long in coming, but she discovered that to be taken seriously in the relatively all-male *holy of holies* in Washington wasn't the easiest thing in the world.

After the first year in politics, however, she couldn't have cared less about Washington. One night while nursing a tumbler of brandy, her eyes suddenly filled with tears and a lump rose in her throat. She *had* to make peace with her daughter, Ann Clare Brokaw.

Ann had grown close to her stepfather, eventually becoming the daughter he never had. Addressing her familiarly as "Annie," Luce signed his frequent letters to his stepdaughter "Dad." But the relationship between mother and daughter was strained, and Ann treated her mother with indifference. When Clare was headed to the West Coast to give a speech, she insisted her daughter join her.

In San Francisco, Clare and Ann spent time together. The two strolled along the city's streets arm in arm. On their route, Ann spotted a Roman Catholic church and she suggested they duck in for a moment of meditation. They stayed through Mass. Clare was strangely touched by the spiritual experience with her daughter.

Ann was a senior at Stanford University and scheduled to

graduate magna cum laude in June. As mother and daughter continued their walk after leaving the church, they discussed Ann's return to college the next morning.

Back at the hotel, the two talked late into the night. Clare insisted she drive her daughter back to school, but Ann had made plans to ride with a friend.

Clare and Ann parted the next morning, each happy in their renewed relationship.

As Ann and her friend traveled to the campus in the open convertible, a car came at them from a side road, sideswiping their car. The convertible spun out of control, hurling Ann out of her seat and into a tree. Death was instantaneous.

Clare started a family cemetery at Mepkin, and Ann Clare Brokaw's body was laid to rest there. As soon as arrangements could be made, Clare had her mother's remains removed from the original resting place and buried at Mepkin with Ann.

The Luce family cemetery at Mepkin Abbey.
Photograph by SID RHYNE.

Clare spent hours under the oaks, gazing at her daughter's grave site. The fact that Ann had asked to pray in the Roman Catholic church the day before her death had a profound effect on Clare. She decided it was time for her to give more thought to spiritual matters and she began to meet with priests.

Clare Boothe Luce was received into the church at St. Patrick's Cathedral February 16, 1946. Her husband said he had always believed she would one day become a Roman Catholic.

Clare and Henry Luce began to talk about the future of Mepkin Plantation. It was agreed that the main house, the four guest houses, and 3,130 acres of land be transferred to the Trappist Order. Clare said the transfer of property seemed the most normal thing in the world, considering the nearest town to the property was called Moncks Corner.

Once the Trappist monks were established at Mepkin, they had virtually a self-sustaining colony, dependent almost entirely on the fruits of their labors. Most of what they ate was grown in their own fields. They shunned modern farm machinery, so labor was generally a manual effort.

This austere Catholic order permitted seven hours of sleep. The monks retired at 7:00 p.m. Each day began at 2:00 a.m.—except on Sundays and special days when they arose even earlier—with the long, pre-dawn vigil of chants and prayers. Breakfast was around daybreak. Daylight hours included much work in the fields, poultry houses, and livestock yards. The Luces continued to keep in touch with the head of the silent monastic order's abbey, although they rarely made visits.

Henry Luce was in residence at his Arizona Biltmore Estates home when he died in February 1967. He had once told Clare that he would like to be laid to rest at Mepkin Abbey if they could find a Presbyterian minister to pray over him. As he requested, Presbyterian rites were held in the family cemetery at the Abbey. The headstone marking his grave is carved in the likeness of a live oak tree. Under the limbs on one side of the marker are the words "Here lies Henry R. Luce, April 3, 1898, February 28, 1967."

Clare bought an oceanfront home in Hawaii but she missed the excitement of Washington, D.C. When she decided to buy an apartment at Watergate Apartments, she was asked for references just like anyone else. She bought three apartments there.

When Clare became ill, Father Christian, the abbot of Mepkin Abbey, visited her. "She was lissome, scintillating, chic, and always the center of attention," he said. Father Christian continued to visit Clare at Watergate Apartments, and when she became very weak he administered last rites. "We talked of theological matters," he said. "I thought she was the prettiest I had ever seen her. The medication had filled out her face, and although her hair was gray, it had a wave. There was a softness to her; her skin looked almost translucent."

Clare Boothe Luce died in October 1987 at the age of 84. Services were scheduled at St. Patrick's Cathedral in New York and St. Stephen Martyr Church in Washington. Father Christian conducted the private burial in the family cemetery at Mepkin. "Here lies Clare Booth Luce" was carved on the remaining side of the headstone that marked the resting place of Henry Luce.

The funeral of Clare Boothe Luce. Father Christian is on far right. Luce family members and friends surround coffin.
Photograph courtesy of FATHER CHRISTIAN, abbot of Mepkin Abbey.

Solomon Guggenheim home at 9 East Battery.
Photograph by SID RHYNE.

Cain Hoy Plantation

Harry G. Guggenheim was introduced to the South Carolina Low Country by his uncle, Solomon Guggenheim. And what an introduction it must have been!

Solomon's house at 9 East Battery in Charleston was sold into the New York dynasty of Guggenheim millionaire modern art patrons by the Seigling family. The feature that attracted Harry most to the home was the large fragment of a Civil War cannon resting in the attic. The prominent reminder of the final days of the bloody conflict was a testimony to the solid construction of the 1838 mansion. Harry made up his mind he too would own some of that Low Country history. He would look for a place where he could keep his horses. Also, he wanted to fish, and the South Carolina Low Country had plenty of water.

The community of Cain Hoy caught Harry Guggenheim's eye.

The village was laid out in 1789 as a summer settlement for Low Country rice planters convinced the air in the pinelands protected them from the *vapours* believed to cause malaria and yellow fever. With a family fortune as large as one could imagine, Harry Guggenheim—who was a partner in the mining firm Guggenheim Brothers; ambassador to Cuba; an aviation pioneer; a Navy veteran in World Wars I and II; publisher of *Newsday*, a Long Island newspaper; and the head of a number of foundations—could make many choices. His great-grandfather had begun building the family fortune in mining after he emigrated to the United States from Switzerland in 1848.

Harry Guggenheim took as his third and last wife a daughter of Joseph Medill Patterson, founder and publisher of the *New York Daily News*, and great-granddaughter of Joseph Medill, founder of the *Chicago Tribune*. Together the couple established *Newsday* in 1940 with Harry as president and Alicia Patterson Guggenheim as editor.

Guggenheim purchased the 15,000-acre Cain Hoy Plantation and set about building a home on the property. "Mr. Guggenheim came to Cain Hoy Plantation by boat up until 1929, when the Cooper River Bridge (John P. Grace Memorial Bridge) was built," said Harold Lincoln, a former hunting guide for Guggenheim, who lives on a nearby twenty-acre tract of land given to his ancestors after the Civil War. "That was the only way the Guggenheims could come in—by boat. They came in at Charleston, passed by Sullivans Island, and on up the Cooper River. You can see the old boathouse at the landing today, where the Guggenheim yacht rode at anchor. After the bridge was built, they came by automobile."

Guggenheim's $250,000 mansion, designed by New York architects Polhemus & Coffin, was painted a cream color and roofed with Ludowici English tile. Old English brick steps and winding iron handrails lead to a pillared portico. Copper hinges and locks at the entrance were a clue to the copper decorative scheme throughout the interior. A handsome living room had a huge open fireplace on the west side. Built into the overmantel was a copper-colored mirror etched with two wild turkeys. Terra cotta light fixtures shaped like lotus leaves hung in the dining room, concealing bare bulbs and providing indirect light. The section of the house occupied by the Guggenheims was paneled entirely in cypress.

"Among my maps and plats of the various parcels of the Cain Hoy Plantation that lie between the Cooper and Wando Rivers, is one dated 1709, which shows the broad path from Thomas Island to Canehay," said Harry Guggenheim. "When I first came to Cain Hoy, I heard the fable of the ferryman named Cain, a ferryman on the Wando River whose customers attracted his attention from across the river by shouting 'Cain Ahoy!'" It was believed by some the name of the village originated with this ferryman.

There is another theory, however, that seems more plausible. As cane, with its succulent palm-like leaf on which cattle feed,

Cain Hoy manor house.
Photograph by SID RHYNE.

is so plentiful in the area, the name "Canehay" was given by the early settlers. It's easy to see how that could have been corrupted over time into *Cain Hoy*.

"On another plat dated 1792 there is a tract deeded to John Primots. This is now included in several hundred acres of small holdings surrounded by my plantation and known as Jack Primous. I suggest that the original land was granted to a French Huguenot, Jean Primot." Guggenheim was to say later, "Of all my material possessions, I am fondest of this place."

Harold Lincoln said that Guggenheim provided the funds for the upkeep of St. Thomas Episcopal Church, built in 1706. The first building was destroyed by fire, and the existing building was erected in 1819. "We call it the Old Brick Church. Mr. Guggenheim gave them a generous donation each year. Yes, sir. They knew that donation was coming."

As sure as the village residents knew Guggenheim would send his donation to the church, Guggenheim knew that guests would come to his plantation each year during hunting season. Among the celebrities who visited Cain Hoy for hunting and relaxation was Gen. James H. (Jimmy) Doolittle, who led the first World War II raid on Tokyo. Doolittle visited the plantation in 1942.

"Senator Harry Byrd came," said Lincoln. "Not the Byrd you hear about now, the old man Senator Byrd." (Harry Flood Byrd became a U.S. senator in 1922. He gained fame for his work on government economy.) "Mr. Guggenheim had about four crews, and a crew went with each group that went hunting. When someone wanted to go fishing, a crew went to the river with them. There was a crew to take you anywhere you wanted to go."

Guggenheim always rose early each morning. For his hunting parties he dressed in proper hunting clothes and his trademark riding boots. His image was striking and, like his industrialist and philanthropist ancestors, Harry Guggenheim appeared larger than life.

Although Guggenheim wanted to get into the cattle business, he was wary of get-rich-quick schemes. "This is no Eldorado where anyone can rush in and make a killing. It takes time and patience," he observed. "You need wells and equipment. You must stock with the very best cattle available. You must have superb operators, people who know the cattle business. I want to gradually build up Daniel's Island into pasture. Of course, we'll leave windbreaks and shade areas but we definitely plan to put the high land into permanent pasturage."

Guggenheim took the time to establish a cattle operation that was carried out on some 1,150 acres of his island's high land. The Cain Hoy Hereford herd was made up of 655 breeder cows and 21 bulls. The calf crop, which was sold as feeders, totaled 542. Four silos were filled with more than 5,000 bales of hay stored for winter food. Guggenheim paid special attention to summer and winter pastures that were composed of clovers and fescue, native grasses, and Dallis grass. He sought the counsel of the famous King Ranch in Texas and at its suggestion tried out Coastal Bermuda.

Guggenheim also gave special attention to his horses. His favorite was Dark Star.

Dark Star was bought by the Cain Hoy Stables from Hermitage Farm near Louisville, where he was bred. Cain Hoy paid $6,500 for the brown colt in 1951.

Before the Kentucky Derby in 1953, Guggenheim was concerned over the possibility of Dark Star's being defeated by Native Dancer, a horse belonging to Alfred Gwynne Vanderbilt, son of Margaret Emerson whose son George Vanderbilt owned Arcadia Plantation. Everyone knew that Alfred Gwynne Vanderbilt had inherited his mother's passion for horses, and he had developed a fine stable. But Dark Star was not to be discredited.

The day of the Derby—Saturday, May 2, 1953—arrived. The horses were led around the owner turn from the backstretch barns. The bands lined up on the infield. Soldiers, sailors, and marines stepped forward in their colors. The big stage was set for the playing of the "Star Spangled Banner" and "My Old Kentucky Home." The horses were in their places. Everything was set for the big moment.

That moment came when starter Ruby White pressed the button to open the flaps in the gate. The race was on.

It wasn't long before spectators noticed the contest was between Dark Star and Native Dancer. All eyes were glued to the course as the two horses breathlessly approached the finish line, traveling neck and neck.

Dark Star won by a nose. He had done it!—over a fast track and under the handling of a young man named Henry Moreno. Guggenheim, holding the lead strap, was ecstatic at the presentation stand, where the rosebuds were draped over his horse. The horse's two-minute, two-second run netted $90,050 for Harry Guggenheim. After the initial excitement of Churchill Downs was over, the proud owner of Dark Star returned to Cain Hoy Plantation to attend his cattle.

"I remember that fine horse in the stable at Cain Hoy Plantation, right here in South Carolina," Harold Lincoln said. "Winning the Kentucky Derby was a big event in Mr. Guggenheim's life, but he came back here and got to work.

"Mr. Guggenheim's interest in the plantation's management, his involvement with the servants, and his accommodating character—that all had a deep effect on people."

Gippy Plantation's Milk Tasted Like Nectar

Nicholas G. Roosevelt of Philadelphia loved Christmas. After he bought Gippy (pronounced "Jippy") Plantation near Moncks Corner in 1927, a Christmas card sent to friends displayed a photograph of the large white house in the oaks. The inscription read, "Merry Christmas, from Emily and Nicholas Roosevelt."

Roosevelt recounted after that holiday that a friend dropped in on Christmas Eve with a package for "each of us, and Georgie brought a thick slice of her three-layer fruit cake. Lockwood and Magdalene called, and Mabel put the final touches on the wreath and hung it on the front door. We had the red candlelight by the window to guide The Spirit in finding Its way to us."

The Spirit had surely found its way to Gippy Plantation and guided the hand of the builder. The magnificent manor house is an extraordinary setting for a Christmas celebration and the perfect image for a greeting card.

Gippy Plantation was originally a portion of the Fairlawn Barony, estate of Sir John Colleton, one of the Lords Proprietors of Carolina. It was purchased in 1821 by John White. White named the plantation after a slave who had a penchant for running away and hiding in a swamp on the tract. The original manor house burned and White rebuilt on the site in 1852.

White, a lieutenant in the Confederate army, died of typhoid fever in 1865. His widow continued to live in the house despite warnings of possible Union army occupation.

The warning soon became reality. Confederate troops passed through the plantation after evacuating Charleston in the spring of 1865. Within a few days northern troops invaded the place.

White's son, J. St. Clair, was but a boy at the time of the incident, and the only male on the premises. In the house with mother and son was a Mrs. Brunson, who was staying with them. The three witnessed the approach of the Union soldiers, who fired on Confederate scouts come to warn of the enemy's approach.

Sherman's troops dismounted and began their usual search. Poultry and all movable supplies were quickly stolen, as were small valuables from the house. The occupants were unmolested, however, and the house itself left intact.

J. St. Clair White inherited the plantation at his mother's death and sold it in 1895 to his cousin, Samuel Gaillard Stoney of Medway Plantation. Stoney moved onto Gippy and planted the land until 1910, when he moved to downtown Charleston.

Old building adjacent to Gippy manor house.
Photograph by SID RHYNE.

Gippy Plantation manor house.
Photograph by SID RHYNE.

The famous Roosevelts were diplomats, authors, and lecturers, but Nicholas chose the life of a gentleman farmer. He set about arranging his estate so he could live and work in comfort.

None of Roosevelt's activities were as dear to his heart as the one that few friends knew interested him: dairy farming. He believed he had finally come full circle and could spend as much time as was necessary indulging in the delight of his heart. With his chest barreled in pride, he started his dairy farm in October 1928 with 80 cows. Forty-one were registered Guernsey milk cows and 39 were good grade cows. The plan was to begin the project with good grade milkers and gradually build up the herd with pure-bred cows, selling off the grades. When registered Guernseys numbered 240, an average of 115 cows were milked.

The dairy's average daily production was more than a thousand quarts. Every quart sold. Several schools in Berkeley County purchased from Gippy for the students, and drug stores and restaurants in town received deliveries each day. The remaining milk was delivered to private individuals in

Charleston. Roosevelt's desire was to produce the best milk the South Carolina Low Country had to offer. What his relatives were to politics, he desired to be to dairy farming in the state of South Carolina. He became much more.

In 1932 Roosevelt bought Foremost's May King, a bull sired by Langwater Foremost, the senior herd sire owned by chain store king J. C. Penny. Langwater Foremost was the sire of eight advanced registered females, each producing as much as forty pounds of milk with her first calf. Valor's County, son of Langwater's Valor, also purchased from Penny, was valued at $25,000.

Incorporating such excellent stock lines, Roosevelt slowly moved his dairy farming into a phase that proved interesting from a scientific standpoint. Eighteen of his milkers were included in a test. The results confirmed that bloodlines counted when it came to breeding animals. One of the cows, Mill Dale Lady Elsie, completed her one-year test with a record production of 18,157 pounds of milk and 728 pounds of butterfat. Much in the manner of the Charleston aristocracy, one might say, Roosevelt's herd was in a class by itself. "My cows are aristocrats," the proud owner crowed.

By 1933, no new cows were being purchased. At that time, Roosevelt's herd was composed of 157 cows, 147 of which were purebred Guernseys.

After Roosevelt had been dairying for twenty years, other plantation owners followed his lead and began raising cattle on their land. None other was awarded the sobriquet "producer of the best milk in the country."

Archibald Rutledge, poet laureate of South Carolina and owner of Hampton Plantation said, "Practically a new thing in the Deep South, dairying has become a foremost industry of the plantations. I believe that Nicholas Roosevelt, at Gippy Plantation on the Cooper River, started all this; and although he began two decades ago, even today the southern eye, drearily accustomed to half-wild and half-starved cattle, is startled by seeing a fine herd of Holsteins, Jerseys, or Guernseys. . . . I personally can testify that after a lifetime of drinking ordinary South Carolina milk, a glass of milk from Roosevelt's dairy tastes like nectar."

Bonnie Doone Plantation

Alfred H. Caspary, a wealthy New Yorker whose father had given him a seat on the New York Stock Exchange at the age of twenty-one, was a visionary. Assembling seven plantations in the South Carolina Low Country, Caspary formed a 14,000-acre hunting preserve. He used an old existing gate as main entrance to the estate and liked to describe the avenue leading to his mansion as "a six-mile drive through a deer park."

At night, as visitors maneuvered down the wooded avenue, the beams of their car's headlights shone on what appeared to be dozens of tiny lights scattered among the trees. On closer examination, one could see that they were not headlights at all, but the eyes of dozens of deer.

The deer were always on the alert, every sense attuned to the surroundings. But their vigilance didn't indicate a readiness to run away. However, when a scent, a sound, a glimpse of the unexpected invaded too closely their space, they would gracefully leap out of sight. Bonnie Doone Plantation was the perfect hunt club.

Caspary hired Rodolphus Alexandra Boodle as private game warden. The first deer hunt was scheduled, and northern friends were invited to accompany Caspary and share in the southern tradition. Great plans were made for the big day.

When the guests had arrived and were settled, horses were made ready. The visitors mounted as Boodle waited, already in his saddle. When all were in place, they set off from the rear of the mansion.

After having ridden only a short distance, a deer crossed the road in front of the hunting party. Boodle shouted to Caspary,

"Shoot, man. Bring down the deer." Caspary leveled his rifle and shot. The deer fell.

Caspary dismounted and ran to the deer. He kneeled for a few minutes by the animal's side before returning to the group.

"Go on with the drive," he said. "I'm not going with you. I've just seen a deer cry."

"You saw a deer cry?" someone asked.

"I did. The deer had tears in its eyes, and it's unlikely I'll ever be able to erase from my mind the picture of those eyes, pleading with me for its life. I've had my first and last deer hunt."

True to his word, Caspary never hunted deer again, but he enjoyed a quiet life on his historic plantation.

William Hopton received a royal land grant of 15,000 acres from King George I in 1722. The history of the plantation between Hopton's ownership and the 1850s is unclear. Many Colleton County records were lost in the destruction of the city of Columbia during the Civil War. Maj. Henry T. Ferguson fell heir to the property and maintained it until his death in 1859. Records show that in 1850 115,000 pounds of rice were produced on the plantation.

In 1861 title to the plantation was in the name of Dr. Theodore De Hon, a son of the Right Reverend De Hon, Bishop of the Episcopal Church and priest of St. Michael's Church in Charleston. The name of the plantation at that time was De Hon. During De Hon's days, Union troops arrived, burned the house and all outbuildings, and carried De Hon to Charleston as a prisoner of war.

After the war, the property was owned by Cotesworth Pinckney Fishburne, who planted 476 acres in rice. Title of ownership changed several times before Caspary purchased the plantation April 27, 1931. Historian Lucius G. Fishburne said that Bonnie Doone was an improper name for the plantation, but the Casparys chose it very likely as a tribute to the first stanza of Robert Burns' poem "The Banks 'o Doon."

> Ye banks and braes o'bonny Doon,
> How can ye bloom sae fresh and fair?
> How can ye chant, ye little birds,
> An I sae wary fu' o' care!

Thou'll break my heart, thou warbling bird,
That wantons thro' the flowering thorn!
Thou minds me o' departed joys,
Departed never to return

After construction of the main house, Caspary commissioned Benito Innocenti, a noted New York landscape architect to design the gardens. A serpentine wall of brick encloses a collection of rare and lovely camellia japonica bushes.

In a recent article, noted landscape architect Robert Marvin is quoted as saying, "The camellia garden is an outstanding attraction to this day." Marvin, who lived on Bonnie Doone Plantation from age seven until he married at twenty-six, is one of the nation's most respected landscape architects. His firm, Robert Marvin & Associates, has won twenty-six national awards, ten of which have been presented by the nation's First Ladies at the White House. "My father, William Robert Marvin, was the plantation superintendent for Mr. Caspary, and we lived in the building that is the guest house today. The Casparys were absolutely wonderful to our family."

According to Marvin, all furnishings in the Bonnie Doone mansion came from Europe. Rooms were filled with a combination of English Queen Anne and Chippendale furniture. Walls were hung with sporting paintings. And the Oriental porcelains were the embodiment of the home of the famous philanthropist and art collector.

Mrs. Caspary's bedroom was a many-windowed room that faced the gardens in back of the mansion. A large tiled bathroom, a dressing room, and many closets completed her suite. Mr. Caspary's bedroom faced the avenue of oaks in front of the house. It consisted of a large bedroom, tiled bathroom, and closets. Floors in the mansion were of hardwood except in the solarium, where stone was used.

In 1938, *House Beautiful* magazine named the living room of the Georgian mansion one of the 100 most beautiful rooms in America.

"Mr. Caspary had a huge vault built within the house," Marvin recalls, "and he spent a lot of time there going over his second-most-valuable-stamp-collection-in-America, and his Rothschild china collection that was from Europe and quite

Bonnie Doone Plantation manor house shortly after the Casparys moved in.
Photograph courtesy of CHARLESTON BAPTIST ASSOCIATION.

The Casparys and their housekeeper, Mrs. Caspary's sister, on the terrace at the back of the mansion.
Photograph courtesy of CHARLESTON BAPTIST ASSOCIATION.

famous, as well as his other collections."

According to a daughter of Caspary's chauffeur Herman, the house servants wore uniforms. Herman wore red knee socks, white knickers, a red jacket, and a white cap.

The butler, from Sweden, was pretty much in charge of everything that went on in the mansion, even though Mrs. Caspary had her maid and a housekeeper.

Mr. Caspary saw that his dogs received the best care. The dog graveyard can be seen today, with white marble gravestones inscribed Spot, Rip, Daffodil, and other names.

The Casparys ate breakfast on the terrace at the back of the house. A little boy named King Solomon, a descendant of slaves, kept the lawn "picked" clean of sticks, leaves, nuts, etc.

Caspary died January 7, 1955, after a long illness. Services were held at Frank L. Campbell, "The Funeral Church," on Madison Avenue at 81st Street in New York. When Mrs. Caspary died, her ashes were scattered over the plantation.

King Solomon grew up and became a noted fishing guide. One of his best friends in later years was Dr. McLeod Frampton, a Presbyterian minister who visited Bonnie Doone

King Solomon, in front of his house on Bonnie Doone Plantation.
Photograph courtesy of CHARLESTON BAPTIST ASSOCIATION.

Plantation often when it was owned by the Presbytery.

"The thing about Sol that was so fascinating was that although he never went to school he was, in his own way, a good teacher of philosophy, theology and psychology," said Frampton.

King Solomon married a woman named Betsy, and they lived on the banks of the Ashepoo River near Bonnie Doone Plantation. One day Dr. Frampton called at the house to request that King Solomon go fishing with him. "He knew every inch of that river," Frampton recounted, "where the fish were, when they were biting, everything."

"Betsy, where is Sol?"

"I ain't know where Sol is."

"Betsy, you don't know where he is? Are you worried about him?" Frampton quizzed the woman.

"No, sir. He'll come back."

"How long has he been gone?"

"About two months."

Frampton went home, and when he next saw King Solomon, he asked him where he had been.

"'Twas fishing with a man, and the man kept me fishing until it was late at night. While I was walking home, a Yankee gentleman came by and stop the car and asked if I want to ride," King Solomon explained. "I sat in the back seat of that car, and it was so warm, I gone right to sleep. When I wake up I been in Florida."

"Why didn't you tell Betsy?" Frampton asked.

"You can't tell somebody where you are iffen you don't know where you are."

King Solomon went on to say that he went to work and made $500. "I took it to the bank and gave it to the man in the cage, and the man asked me my name. 'Solomon.' Then he asked me what my first name was. 'King.'"

The man left the cage and took King Solomon's money into a bank vault. The following day Solomon went to the man in the cage and asked to see his money. He was escorted to the vault and shown a stack of bills.

The next day King Solomon went back to the bank and asked to see his money, just to see if it was still there. The banker insisted that Solomon take his money and leave with it.

"Rev," King Solomon said to Dr. Frampton, "I put that money under my pillow that night, and somebody steal it."

"What did you do then?"

"I walk home, all the way back to Bonnie Doone Plantation."

"Wasn't that an awfully long walk?" Frampton questioned.

"No, sir," King Solomon answered. "I was walking back *home.*"

Bonnie Doone Plantation house.
Photograph by SID RHYNE.

Prospect Hill Plantation

Barbara Hutton was one of those women whose silky hair fell with indifference to her shoulders, whose features were uniform and shapely, whose skin was perfect, and whose phonograph record eyes scooped you in or pushed you back. She could have been a film star but they don't make roles for women who look that cultured.

Throughout her adult life she was carried back to childhood by the extravagant bed sheets custom-made for her by Madame Porthault. All in white, Douanier Rouseau's jungle scenes were meticulously hand embroidered on the fold-back in full relief. The exaggerated forms of roaring lions, tigers, and jungle-like palms and leaves were much like the house decor and landscape of her father's home, Curley Hut, on his South Carolina plantation, Prospect Hill. The tropical foliage, the Zebra Room, the plantation wildlife—all had made a vivid impression on Barbara. Her hazel eyes traced the design of the Porthault sheets and pillow cases as she lay in bed during the last years of her life. Her anguished mind raced back to Prospect Hill Plantation on the Edisto River.

Back home, palms dotted the swamps and forests; azaleas burst into sudden blazes of red and purple on the lawn; bamboo grew to enormous circumference; and alligators bellowed in the night.

The Zebra Room was that of her father. The furniture was upholstered in zebra skins. The rugs were made of the skins of other animals. Many horned heads and varied species of preserved waterfowl were mounted on the walls. The jungle scenes that had been embroidered by Madame Porthault were actually scenes etched on Barbara's mind from winters she'd spent at Prospect Hill Plantation on Yonges Island.

The Hutton estate was elaborately decorated. It was a playground for young and old alike.

Even the Huttons' dog kennels were elaborate. In fact, they once caused a dispute between a newspaper reporter and the islanders. Chlotilde R. Martin of Beaufort spent many days working on an article about the Huttons. During her research, she called at the homes of many islanders, some of whom invited her to partake of delicious meals. Without exception, the islanders commented on the Hutton's luxurious kennels.

The Martin newspaper article revealed that each dog lived in a two-room suite with a bed built off the floor and its own private food dish. "None of these people could believe it when they heard that such a fine house had been built for dogs, so the entire countryside went to see for itself," Martin wrote. "And it still gets goggle-eyed when it talks about those dog kennels."

The islanders objected to Martin's description of the people in the region as "simple Low Country neighbors, and their goggle-eyed interest in the handsome dog kennels." Martin later printed an apology to all the people of Willtown Bluff.

Prospect Hill manor house.
Photograph by SID RHYNE.

Although land records were destroyed during the Civil War, it is believed that Edward Barnwell bought Prospect Hill from Hannah Hasell in 1835. Four years later Barnwell produced 180,000 pounds of rice on the plantation, which was located on the east side of the Edisto River near Willtown.

Barnwell married wealthy Margaret Manigault in 1835, with whom he had seventeen children. Margaret died at the age of forty-four, when their youngest child was only two.

After Barnwell's death in 1885 the property was sold at auction. A relative bought it in 1890, and he leased one acre of land to the trustees of the AME church of Adams Run, a nearby village. The lease agreement was to run for ninety-nine years at the rate of one cent a year.

Theodore Ravenel acquired Prospect Hill in 1894, and title changed again before E. F. Hutton bought the property that was conveyed to his brother, Franklyn L. Hutton, October 31, 1929.

A story is told by Jack Leland, former editor of the *Charleston Evening Post*, about the Halloween transaction, which not only included Prospect Hill Plantation but several tracts grouped as

Avenue of oaks leading to manor house.
Photograph by SID RHYNE.

Oakhurst islands, as well as others. Franklyn Hutton arrived at the lawyer's office. As they considered a certain tract, he slammed his hat on the table and said to the party handling the closing, "I'll give you $25,000 for that plantation."

"I'll take it," the other party replied.

Papers were drawn up and as Hutton handed over the check, he said, "All southerners are fools. I'd have paid you $50,000 just as quickly as I paid you $25,000."

The other man thought about that for a moment, then answered, "Mr. Hutton, all northerners are fools. I'd have taken $5,000 as quickly as I took $25,000."

The original plantation manor house at Prospect Hill was no longer in existence. The house built by Edward Barnwell to replace the one burned during the Civil War stood at the end of an avenue of moss-draped oaks. At the time Hutton obtained the property, the house was inhabited by the plantation's caretaker. As Hutton considered that house established as the caretaker's residence, he decided to build a new house for his family.

The site of an old rice mill was selected for the new mansion. When the house was completed, it resembled something you might expect to see in parts of Africa—more rugged beauty than aristocratic splendor.

A large front porch with six columns faced the river. The inland entrance was French Colonial in style with a small rounded porch and two columns. The thirty-room house had nine bedrooms. Most of the home's walls were of old brick, while the remaining were of varied types of wood paneling. A majority of rooms had exposed beams.

Many rooms were adorned with fireplaces large enough to accommodate cooking an ox and racks filled with various kinds and sizes of guns. Even the breakfast room had a gun rack.

A large grandfather clock stood in the entrance hall near the stairway. From the hall one entered the huge living room, where deep plush carpets were arranged on the wood floors. At least two dozen animal heads were mounted on the walls on a panel than ran above the family portraits. The room exuded a feeling of being in Africa, where Cape buffalo, zebra, and wildebeest roam. The variety of furniture materials and design would have made cheetahs, lions, and leopards—as well as their foes and prey—feel right at home. A swordfish hung above a fireplace, between antlers of African animals.

The dining room had built-in corner cupboards. Bedrooms were furnished with traditional four-poster beds. Bathrooms were outfitted with physical therapy equipment: electric heat cabinets, massage tables, and glass enclosed tubs with two seats.

Behind the house, deer, duck, and quail were in abundance. A boat landing and a boathouse were set up at that point on the river for visitors' yachts and fishing boats. The Hutton yacht and private railroad car were named Curley Hut.

Jack Leland remembered Barbara Hutton. "Barbara was fat as a teenager. Her father hired the world's best rifleman, a man of German extraction, who lived in Charleston. He supervised the care of the horses and was the hunting guide. There was a huge barn and stable on the plantation, and that is where he stayed.

"Barbara fell in love with the rifleman and desired him to be *her* groom, but her father would have none of it. Girls in her social position didn't fall in love with common people, they believed."

Barbara went on to marry a count, a prince, and actor Gary Grant, but she was never happy. People around Prospect Hill Plantation believe that had she married the rifleman, she would have had a happier life.

Barbara Hutton often visited her cousin, the beautiful actress Dina Merrill, when they were young. Dina was the daughter of the E. F. Huttons who owned Laurel Spring Plantation, near Prospect Hill.

Although Barbara Hutton had seen great wealth during her lifetime, she was financially drained at the time of her death. In a recent interview on *Larry King Live*, Dina Merrill, a well-publicized philanthropist, commented how unfortunate it was that, considering the wealth her cousin enjoyed, she had not chosen to give something back to the world.

Laurel Spring Plantation

"Marjorie Merriweather Post was the
richest woman in the world. Mar-A-Lago,
the home she built in Palm Beach, is
the most magnificent estate in North and
South America. She spent $20 million
on the house during its construction
from 1920 to 1928."

—Donald Trump
Present Owner of Mar-A-Lago

Marjorie Merriweather Post Hutton built her famous house in Palm Beach during the time she and her husband, Edward Francis (E. F.) Hutton, owned Laurel Spring Plantation in South Carolina.

Hutton used Laurel Hill, located on the Combahee River, as a hunting preserve, but he enjoyed the history his plantation afforded.

Laurel Spring was first owned by the Lynah family. To the right of the house is the tomb of Dr. James Lynah (1775-1809), who at one time was physician-general of all military hospitals in South Carolina. He is said to have attended Count Pulaski, "a gallant Pole" as historian Simms called him, who came down from the North in 1778 to be of service after Savannah was captured.

Another owner of Laurel Spring was Charles Tidyman Lowndes who served four terms in the South Carolina House of Representatives. Records indicate that in 1860 Lowndes produced nearly two million pounds of rice on the plantation, but by 1866, title had changed to Rawlins Lowndes.

When T. D. Ravenel became owner of the plantation, he planted 700 acres in rice and continued to produce until 1926. E. F. Hutton purchased at least eight plantations from Ravenel, Laurel Spring and Oakland among the eight. Hutton's total properties comprised some 10,000 acres in Colleton County.

The Oakland Plantation house is believed to be the only antebellum home on the Combahee (pronounced "Coomby" by the natives) River spared from the torch during Sherman's march. It seems appropriate that the house was built of cypress, which is called "the everlasting wood." The plantation gardens were famous for the multitude of japonicas and jonquils, planted there by Dr. Drayton Grimke, a friend of the Lowndes family.

In 1931, Daddy Scipio, an aged slave, still lived in one of the houses in "the street," as the row of old slave houses was called. He told a graphic story about a time when the grounds around the Lowndes house at Oakland was strewn with bodies

Riverside view of Hutton lodge.
Photograph by SID RHYNE.

of dead Civil War soldiers whom, he said, were dug up and moved to the National Cemetery in Beaufort. Asked how old he was at that time, Daddy Scipio shook his head. "We been so busy dose days we couldn't keep score of chillun's age." When questioned as to the age of the Lowndes house at Oakland, he replied: "When I had sense, dat house been dere."

Although money was scarce and he begged visitors for a dime with which to buy tobacco, Daddy Scipio defied poverty, jauntily wearing a high silk hat.

E. F. Hutton, who was a close friend of Bernard Baruch and whose history in business was much the same as Baruch's, had started work at $5 a week as a grease monkey and went on to make millions on the stock market. He founded the Wall Street firm that bears his name today.

Hutton's first wife, Blanche Horton, died in 1918. Their only son died two years later. On July 7, 1920, he married Marjorie Merriweather Post Close, daughter and heir of Charles W. Post, founder of the Postum Cereal Company. The Huttons had one daughter, Nedenia, who is known today as Dina Merrill, actress and philanthropist.

Marjorie inherited the bulk of the C. W. Post fortune, including the cereal company. After their marriage, Hutton took a leave of absence from his own company and assumed management of the Postum Cereal Company, which had fallen on hard times. Hutton turned the company around. Postum merged with fourteen grocery companies, forming General Foods. There seemed no end to the money being made.

The Huttons made regular visits to Laurel Spring for hunting parties, traveling by private railroad car. The plantation was a sportsman's paradise and Hutton kept a large number of hunting dogs, always eager to accompany the hunters. As in the manner of his brother Franklyn, his dogs enjoyed fine homes. In fact, both his horses and dogs were privileged animals.

When the weather was clear, the Huttons and their guests hunted duck. Quail were also abundant on the property. Numerous coops were set up for the raising of quail, and hundreds of the fowl were cared for. They were later released into the woods, offering a veritable feast for the hunter.

On rainy days, the hunting party shot skeet.

In 1934 a fire raged in the plantation's marshes. Strong winds carried flames into the oaks and Spanish moss. Burning limbs fell on the roof of the Hutton's lodge. The house was destroyed.

By 1935 a new twenty-room, Z-shaped lodge had been built in its place. The brick sructure, which was painted white, fit perfectly among the beautiful trees, camellias, and azaleas. A wide green lawn swept down from the house to the canal leading to the Combahee River. Although the structure was new, it appeared to have been there for years.

Hutton owned about seventeen miles of river bank and approximately 2,000 acres of rice field, which was said to furnish the best duck shooting of any estate along the coast. On good days the ducks could be seen backed up for half a mile, the water literally black with them. At one point Hutton was accused of sending power boats at night up the Combahee River to frighten ducks away from neighbors' rice fields to the advantage of his own shooting grounds. In retaliation of the

Dog kennels.
Photograph by SID RHYNE.

charges, some property owners set off fireworks to frighten ducks away from Hutton's feeding grounds. In an editorial in a Charleston newspaper just after the incident, Hutton was praised for his excellent contribution to the cause of waterfowl conservation. After that, nothing further was heard of the matter.

In 1935 the marriage between E. F. Hutton and Marjorie Post ended in divorce. Nedenia was twelve. Hutton resigned as chairman of General Foods.

Marjorie Hutton owned several homes: Hillwood in Washington, D.C.; Mar-A-Lago in Palm Beach; and Camp Topridge in the Adirondacks, an estate cared for by sixty-five servants. She traveled extensively—sometimes on her blue Viscount plane, which boasted three pilots and a steward—and she entertained lavishly.

Marjorie remarried in 1936 to Joseph E. Davies, U.S. ambassador to the U.S.S.R. and Belgium. That same year, E. F. Hutton married Dorothy Dear Metzger in Walterboro, South Carolina. Dorothy was divorced from Homer P. Metzger, whom she had married in 1926.

E. F. Hutton died July 11, 1962, at his home, Hutfield, on Wheatly Road in Westbury, Long Island. He was 88. His widow, Dorothy, conveyed to Oswald and Norris Lightsey about ten South Carolina plantations, including Laurel Spring.

Marjorie Merriweather Post Close Hutton Davies died in 1973.

Today, the name Lightsey is displayed at the plantation gate.

Bonny Hall Plantation

Bonny Hall Plantation on the Combahee River was purchased during the 1930s by Nelson Doubleday, son of the founder of the Doubleday book publishing firm in Garden City, New York. At the time of the purchase, young Nelson Doubleday was in charge of the family publishing firm. He had taken over in 1929 when his father became ill. The elder Doubleday died January 30, 1934.

Bonny Hall Plantation, near the small town of Yemassee, South Carolina, comprised some 1,800 acres. It was owned by I. Arthur Lyman of Boston until his death shortly before the Doubleday purchase. The plantation was originally the home of Joseph Blake of England, who never saw it. Blake's son, Walter, planted it until the Civil War. The prosperous Blakes produced over two million pounds of rice in 1859.

The main house was burned during the Civil War, when General Sherman's army marched through the district. It appears the house was looted before being burned, as the Blake family portraits showed up at a sale in New York City two years later. Another house was constructed on the site.

There is a record stating that Bonny Hall was put up for sale on the courthouse steps in Beaufort in 1868 and only a single bid of thirty dollars was made for it. By some means, the Blake family retained possession until it was sold in 1872.

Title to the property changed hands several times. It was owned by George W. Egan, builder of the jetties at the entrance to Charleston Harbor. Egan constructed the central portion of the dwelling presently on the property. Arthur Lyman owned it some time after Egan. In 1934 the executors of the estate of

Lyman transferred ownership of the plantation to Ellen McCarter Doubleday, wife of publisher Nelson Doubleday of New York, for $35,000.

Doubleday completely remodeled the old home. The $30,000 remodeling job and rehabilitation of the old house was completed in 1936. The work was handled by two Charleston firms: Simons & Lapham, architects, and Dawson Engineering Company.

The entire interior of the old house was removed and rebuilt. A two-story wing was added at either side. The west wing, used as servants' quarters, included three bedrooms, two large storerooms, a kitchen, a pantry, and a bath. The master's wing, on the east side, contained on the first floor a bedroom, dressing room, and bath; and on the second floor, two bedrooms and a bath.

On the first floor of the house's main section was a living room, dining room, smoking room, and gun room. The gun room was paneled in cypress. The smoking room was papered

Bonny Hall Plantation house.
Photograph by SID RHYNE.

Barn on Bonny Hall Plantation.
Photograph by SID RHYNE.

in a pine paper, resembling paneling, and the woodwork was painted an old red, brilliantly contrasting the pine. On the second floor were four bedrooms and two baths. The attic contained one large room, capable of quartering a huge hunting party, and a bath.

Cypress weatherboarding, used on the home's exterior, was painted white; the shutters, a dark green. The roof was constructed of slate. A brick terrace with iron handrails adorned the south side of the house. The lawn surrounding the house was planted in winter grass, which showed the house off to advantage. Doubleday hired Umberto Innocenti, noted landscape architect, to design the garden.

In addition to the dwelling itself, the old stables were remodeled and kennels built to house a large pack of hunting dogs. Duck hunting was unusually good at Bonny Hall and partridges were abundant.

A canal was cut to make the house easily accessible by water from the Combahee River. Drinking water was supplied from a flowing artesian well. Doubleday installed his own power plant.

Nelson Doubleday was publisher for the works of author William Somerset Maugham. Doubleday built a comfortable eight-room house on the property to be used by Maugham while writing *The Razor's Edge* (published in 1944). The home's numerous windows provided lovely views of the huge marsh in front and the forest behind.

In addition to the house, the Doubledays gave Maugham a horse and provided a guide who directed the author where to ride and saw that no harm came to him. A gardener kept the landscaped grounds in perfect condition. Two of Doubleday's maids were consigned to take care of preparing meals and cleaning Maugham's house. The staff told acquaintances that Maugham was the funniest man they had ever met. The author seemed equally amused by the area natives. He remarked on their dialect, pointing specifically to the use of "Coomby" for Combahee River, saying he had believed only the British pronounced place names differently from the way they were spelled.

When friends came to visit, Maugham took them to dine with Ellen and Nelson Doubleday and their family in what they all called "the big house." Among friends invited were Dorothy Parker and Jerry Zipkin. There was always a large party at the big house on New Year's Eve, and Maugham usually remained there until the singing of "Auld Lang Syne," which ended the evening.

Maugham accompanied the Doubledays to parties at other

Parker's Ferry, where Maugham wrote *The Razor's Edge*.
Photograph by SID RHYNE.

plantations, and he stared hard through his monocle as he answered questions. Having published books that sold in the tens of millions of copies, he was a celebrity. As much as Maugham liked to write at his new plantation home, he traveled frequently, especially after the weather turned hot in South Carolina. But he always returned.

The Doubledays hunted, fished, and entertained at their plantation until the death of Nelson Doubleday on January 11, 1949. Later that same year, Ellen McCarter Doubleday sold Bonny Hall Plantation to Robert A. Carter and Melvin O. Lane. A 1957 deed revealed that Bonny Hall Plantation was sold to Nicholas G. Penniman III and Martha S. Penniman of Baltimore for $122,600. In 1995, the part of Bonny Hall containing the Doubleday residence was owned by Mr. and Mrs. John Cowperthwaite.

Somerset Maugham, born in 1874, died in 1965. The dean of King's School conducted the committal service. A plaque of stone was placed in the wall of a library located near the grave.

WILLIAM SOMERSET MAUGHAM
K.S.C. 1885–1889
BORN 1874 – DIED 1965

(K.S.C. is abbreviation for King's School, Canterbury)

Richard Taylor now owns the house where Maugham stayed and about fifty acres surrounding it. The place was renamed Parker's Ferry Plantation.

Cherokee Plantation

The South Carolina Low Country rumor mill buzzed in 1969 when it was announced that Aristotle and Jacqueline Kennedy Onassis were negotiating to purchase Cherokee Plantation, a 1,300-acre estate in Colleton County.

The ultra-wealthy Onassis and his new bride, widow of President John F. Kennedy, planned, it was said, to buy property somewhere in South Carolina. Reliable sources in Colleton and Dorchester Counties reported that attorneys had drawn contracts for the purchase of Cherokee Plantation, and the paperwork would reach the Colleton County courthouse for recording within a few days.

The plantation, located on the Combahee River, included a spacious thirty-one-room Georgian mansion flanked by outbuildings and stables. Mrs. Onassis and her children enjoyed riding horses, and the plantation was perfect for that. Mrs. Onassis loved history and had been infatuated with Old South plantations for years. The house's pedigree was perfect for someone of Mrs. Onassis's stature and breeding, and the horse trails, grounds, and woods offered a recreational paradise. The gentle pace of an eighteenth-century plantation seemed to be the perfect setting for this twentieth-century family, and Cherokee would definitely stand up to the family's high standards.

Board House, as Cherokee Plantation was originally known, had been the home of the Blake family. In the manner of many plantation sons, Daniel Blake received his education at Cambridge. He inherited Board House when his father died in 1803. He married Anne Louisa, a member of the noted Middleton family, and set about the huge task of running a plantation. Board House was prosperous and more than a million pounds of rice was produced in 1860.

The main house and outbuildings were destroyed by fire during the Civil War, but some slave homes remained standing. At Daniel's death, his son Dr. Frederick Blake, who had also married a Middleton, owned the property.

William R. and Caroline Coe, of Long Island, New York, purchased Board House from the Blake heirs in 1930 and changed the name to Cherokee Plantation, to honor the Cherokee rose that grew abundantly in the woods. The Olmstead landscape firm, best remembered for designing Central Park in New York City and the grounds of the Biltmore Estate near Asheville, North Carolina, designed the Cherokee Plantation grounds.

The plan was spectacular, and few people will ever forget their first visit to Cherokee, which appears much like a huge park. The initial sense of wonder comes at the first gate, where the name is announced in a design that includes the image of

Entrance to mansion.
Photograph by SID RHYNE.

an American Indian. Proceeding from there toward the mansion, one sees yellow jessamine, Cherokee rose, and wisteria growing among the trees. White fences enclose lawns and pastures where thoroughbred horses graze. When the house comes into view, another gate indicates the driveway, and that leads the visitor through what might be considered yet another gateway: two huge sculptures of lions. The mansion stands out dramatically against the backdrop of blue sky, open pastures, and woods.

The home is entered through large wooden doors. Three of the front rooms once graced castles in Europe. Coe sent architects to Europe to scout the old castles. They returned with three eighteenth-century paneled rooms and several fireplaces and doors. Each of the adjoining rooms was carefully planned and decorated for luxurious and gracious living, and the furnishings and woodwork blend perfectly, achieving a completely harmonious effect.

The house is flanked on each side by an additional wing, extending the length of the structure to more than 130 feet.

William Coe enjoyed hunting, and his plantation abounded in quail, turkey, deer, and other native game, as well as ducks and geese during the winter months. He had a special interest in birds. One day Percy K. Hudson, who owned neighboring Clay Hall Plantation, killed a bird while hunting in woods about seven and a half miles from Cherokee. The bird was banded as belonging to Coe, so Hudson returned it to him. Coe said he had let it loose along with a flock of a hundred birds, and he considered it remarkable the bird roamed so far away from home.

After Coe's death, the plantation was sold to Williams Furniture Corporation of Sumter, a timber company that turned the property into a hunt club. Including other acreage owned by this company, J. T. Buxton, president of Williams Furniture Corporation, said his investment represented about $1.5 million. Buxton announced that the Cherokee Plantation home, all accessory buildings, and approximately 900 acres surrounding the house would be offered for sale. The purchaser would be given the privilege of leasing the hunting rights on the remaining acreage.

The house remained empty until 1956 when R. L. Huffines,

Cherokee Plantation house.
Photograph by SID RHYNE.

Jr., president of Burlington Industries, bought the plantation and restored it to its original grandeur. Huffines, who was also on the Board of ABC-TV, lived at the plantation with his family and developed a horse-breeding farm there. Riding and hunting were popular activities for Huffines' guests, who included Phil Harris, Joan Crawford, and Bing Crosby.

"Cherokee Plantation was paradise for a child," said Calvert W. Huffines, a son of the plantation's owner. "My family would travel during the summer to a more pleasant climate, but I never left. Either the bass were biting or the ducks were flying. There was always something going on that made me want to stay."

When Huffines was contacted with questions about the Onassis offer for the property, he denied reports that Onassis was preparing to buy his plantation. All of the information that had been reported in the Charleston newspapers was false, he said.

In 1969, Huffines sold the property to Robert Beverly Evans, a Detroit industrialist. Evans, a director and member of the executive committee of American Motors and the largest individual stockholder in the company, said he planned to operate the plantation as a cattle farm. He also announced that the plantation house would be redecorated and refurnished.

In 1987, Calvert Huffines was living in Walterboro, where his real estate business specialized in the selling of plantations. At that time Cherokee was owned by the Nerlich Corporation, a Netherlands Antilles Corporation. N. V. Nerlich had started a state-of-the-art hog production company on the plantation. When Nerlich filed Chapter 11 of the Federal Bankruptcy Act, Huffines handled the sale of the property to J. Randolph Updyke, a sportsman from Philadelphia, for $5 million.

Carol and Randolph Updyke had dreamed of owning the beautiful plantation but believed it would never be theirs. While reading the biography of Bernard Baruch, Updyke had set his sights on plantation living. The lifestyle at Baruch's Hobcaw Barony sounded wonderful. The couple had once seen

Lion at last entrance to mansion.
Photograph by SID RHYNE.

Cherokee Plantation included in an old Sotheby's brochure, but by the time they called the broker, it had sold. Alas, four years later it came on the market again. This time, the Updykes bought it.

The property had become run-down and a massive restoration was necessary. The new owners commissioned Bennett and Judie Weinstock, Philadelphia designers who had worked on the Updykes' main residence in Chestnut Hill, Pennsylvania. After three and a half years, the work was completed. "We have redone virtually everything," Updyke said.

Weinstock commented on the dining room. "The splendor derives in part from the wallpaper mural, which relates to the stages of the hunt, an appropriate theme for most Low Country plantations." When Coe was building the mansion in 1931, the huge epic was copied by hand from an original in London's Victoria and Albert Museum, and installed in the house. By the time of the Updike purchase, it was in disrepair. The mural was perfectly restored—not by the Smithsonian but by a local craftsman.

Cherokee Plantation, a landmark—and possibly the *perfect* plantation home—has recently been sold again.

Buckfield Plantation

About the turn of the twentieth century, C. W. Kress, brother of Samuel Henry Kress who owned the chain of "five-and-dimes," bought several plantations that lay primarily in the old Tomotley Barony. Much of the property was originally owned by the McPherson family, and later by the Reverend Gourlay; still later by the Heyward family. The Heywards owned so many plantations throughout the early history of the state it isn't surprising to see that name today in plantation histories regarding the lines of title.

When Buckfield Plantation was owned by the Heywards, it was known as Spotsylvania. That name is remembered particularly for an eyewitness account of the onslaught of General Sherman's troops during the Civil War.

About ten days before Sherman's arrival, it is told, all plantation homes in the parish were intact, even though some of the residents had fled for their safety. Within days, a Confederate scout, hiding at Spotsylvania, watched the Yankees as they tried to take a magnificent barouche from a carriage house. The carriage proved too unwieldy to be moved away, and the soldiers pushed it back inside the carriage house and set the house on fire.

Kress named his entire holdings Buckfield Lodge, a name he obviously took from early maps on which a portion of the property is shown as Buckfield. The old rice fields proved priceless to Kress, so suitable were they for bulb culture. Kress eventually had the largest acreage of white narcissus in the world—1,500 acres—which was very important to his brother, Samuel Henry.

Samuel Henry Kress was born July 23, 1863, in Cherryville, Pennsylvania. He became a teacher, and with money saved from his salary, he purchased a stationery store in Nanticote, Pennsylvania, in 1887. Nine years later he bought a second store, and then opened variety stores in other cities. By consistently reinvesting his income he had acquired twelve stores by 1900.

The chain of Kress stores offered lower prices than most other variety stores at the time. Kress purchased goods directly from manufacturers, then sold them for substantially less than competitors and relied on sales volume to make up for the lower profit margin.

By 1907 Kress had moved his headquarters to New York City and was operating 51 stores. His chain grew to include 264 stores selling $169 million worth of merchandise annually.

In 1921 Kress traveled to Europe, collecting medieval and Renaissance paintings, sculpture, and textiles. His art broker was Joseph Duveen, the same man Mrs. Collis P. Huntington

Buckfield Plantation house.
Photograph by SID RHYNE.

used to acquire her fabulous collection. Duveen said he met two men whom he was to help become collectors almost as great as he was: Mellon, the founder of the National Gallery of Art in Washington, D.C., and Kress, the National Gallery's most lavish contributor. In 1939 Kress gave the newly established National Gallery 375 paintings and 18 sculptures valued at $25 million.

The Kress Foundation, established in 1929, was endowed with forty percent of the S. H. Kress Company's voting stock. The foundation worked in states where Kress stores were in operation. Through the foundation, Kress made million-dollar contributions to medical centers.

Buckfield Lodge gave work to poor people in Jasper County. Flat-bed trucks went into nearby villages before daylight each morning and called for people to come and work in the flower beds. The workers were taken home after dark. Some of them worked in the narcissus beds, and others were taken to several buildings where the bulbs were sorted and packaged for loading on trains. A railroad station known as Kress Station was constructed, and train tracks ran right up to the buildings where the bulbs were packaged and dispatched.

C. W. Kress owned a big German automobile, and he drove over the land, watching as dozens of workers planted and harvested the bulbs, then packed them for shipment by train to the Kress stores. Some stores sold fresh narcissus, and those flowers were prepared for shipping with special care.

Kress lived in a white house of many rooms, and he built an elaborate house for each of his two daughters near his mansion. He took time from his work to hunt with Buckfield guests. Quail were raised on the plantation to serve as prey for the hunters. Quail eggs were incubated. When they hatched, the quail were turned loose in the woods. On rainy days, guests enjoyed shooting skeet.

The Kress daughters are now deceased, and today Buckfield Plantation is utilized for timber production and deer hunting. Each year six hundred acres are planted in long leaf and loblolly pine. Weekends from November to January the land is reserved for use by clients of the present owner for deer hunting. The mansion houses the hunting parties.

A Frenchman Was Watching

James Fripp's life did not lack for the dramatist's sense of timing.

James thought that his future was settled, but when he arrived at Beaufort at the end of the Civil War, he found his dazzling house being sold for taxes.

How he loved that house! All the time he'd been away, he'd felt that a part of his spirit had stayed at home. He had been in brutal skirmishes, had lived through conditions that were all but unbearable, and now his house was being taken from him.

Many people had gathered at the house, and as the auction proceedings got underway, a Frenchman was watching.

The bidding started. In an effort to increase the bids, the auctioneer praised the house.

"You can see that the dwelling sits high off the ground," the auctioneer said. "And don't fail to take into consideration that this place is almost encircled by the Beaufort River. From almost every window you get an extraordinary view."

The Frenchman drew a sigh and walked over to James Fripp. "This is your house?"

"Yes."

"I concluded as much. It shows in your face. Do you not intend to make a bid?"

"It would cost a fortune, and I have nothing," James answered. Striving to control his shaking limbs, he added, "Isn't it by fatal chance that I returned to Beaufort at this very moment?"

"It *is* curious," the Frenchman answered. "You look as if you've lost your last friend."

"Precisely. That is what is happening to me," James answered. "It's an omen. That my house had to be sold for taxes is repugnant enough, but for me to arrive at the very moment of sale is more than I can bear."

"I do not believe it to be an omen," the Frenchman said mechanically. "It's happening everywhere in the South."

The auctioneer never looked toward James Fripp and the Frenchman as he spoke, and it was obvious that he did not know that the owner was in the audience. "Edgar Fripp, a brother of the present owner, built the house," he droned. He threw his hands out in an expansive gesture, as he described how Edgar Fripp had built the large, Italianate-style frame house as his summer home. He had come there to avoid the heat and mosquitos that made life miserable on his plantation across the river, on Saint Helena

Tidalholm, the Fripp house, and the location of the filming of the movies The Great Santini *and* The Big Chill.
Photograph by SID RHYNE.

Island. As the auctioneer reached for the deed and turned it over in his hands, the bidding resumed.

"While I was away, in battle, my mind was seldom far from this house," James said to the Frenchman. "There were many things that I pictured in my mind: sunlight on the rippling water, my books, the garret room, the double portico, the breeze from the river . . . The picture of my house was always with me."

"Your family, was it an old one?" the Frenchman asked.

"The Fripps were planting on Saint Helena Island by 1725," James answered. "They reinvested their assets until their holdings included more than twelve thousand acres on the islands that surround this town. My ancestors were the largest landholders in the parish."

"This magnificent house has a handsome hall and stairway," the auctioneer continued, describing the exceptional cornice work in the larger rooms; the woodwork over the doors and windows, which was reeded with medallions at each corner; the special plaster cornice that looked like paper lace.

"Please, just for a moment," the Frenchman begged of James, his eyes soft and imploring, "tell me something of your experience in battle."

James took a step closer to the house, and said with deadly coldness, "We were painfully exposed. We needed protection."

"Speak no more. The memory tortures you," the Frenchman cried, his mind frozen at the idea of James on the battlefields.

"Do I hear another bid?" the auctioneer shouted.

"I raise the last bid by two thousand dollars," the Frenchman shouted. No one took his challenge. The house was his.

The audience stirred and whispered, wondering who this new owner was. No one seemed to know him, but they had heard that a Frenchman had arrived in town, and surely this was the man. It was their observation that he had chosen the perfect house for his residence.

The Frenchman walked to the steps and stood under an oak tree. He removed a large sum of money from a pouch and counted out the correct sum.

James stood perfectly still. Not even an eyelash flickered.

When the deed was given to the Frenchman, he walked over to James. After kissing him on both cheeks, he handed him the document. "The house is yours."

For a moment the words didn't sink into James' befuddled mind. He continued to stare at the Frenchman uncomprehendingly, and then, as if a veil had been magically lifted, he stammered, "You . . . you don't mean . . . what have you done?"

"For the whole world I would not have missed being here today and buying the house for you," the Frenchman answered.

James blinked and shook his head vigorously. He wanted to put his arms around the Frenchman's neck and hug him.

"Don't try to thank me. I have received my reward," the Frenchman said. "And, James, accept a word of wisdom. You *deserve* to own the Fripp house. Remove from your mind any thoughts of restitution, redemption and humiliation. I came here to assist in the cause of the South. Although my arrival was late, I feel that I have accomplished my mission." Having said that, the Frenchman left quickly, never to be heard from again.

When Pat Conroy's book *The Great Santini* was filmed, Tidalholm, the Fripp House, was selected as the location for the Bing Crosby-Warner Brothers movie. It was the perfect place to film the story, based on Conroy's childhood in Beaufort, where he lived with his family, including his Marine pilot father. The Beaufort Marine Corps Air Station is located near the town, and the U.S. Marine Base at Parris Island is nearby. Another movie, *The Big Chill*, was also filmed at the Fripp House.

The Walls That Refused To Fall

The ruins of Old Sheldon Church, just off U.S. 21 and U.S. 17 about 17 miles north of Beaufort, are testimony that this church was once one of the handsomest in South Carolina. A clergyman once wrote that Sheldon Episcopal Church was more beautiful than St. Philip's and more elegant than St. Michael's, Charleston churches that are known for their beauty and elegance.

Sheldon Episcopal Church had been paid for by 1757, for that was the year of its consecration. According to the canons of the Church of England, consecration services could not be held until there was no debt on the church. During the Revolutionary War, in May 1779, General Augustine Prevost and his British troops burned the building, but the walls refused to give in. The church was restored in 1827. Then, in February 1865, when Sherman's troops were marching from Savannah to Columbia, the church was again burned, but its massive brick walls survived. Many of South Carolina's noblest families have worshipped within those walls, which have withstood turbulent wars, economic ruptures and the ravages of time.

The Bull family figured prominently in the history of Old Sheldon Church and South Carolina. The Bull estate, close to the church, was called Sheldon Hall, after the family's ancestral home in England.

In *Visitations of Warwick, 1682–1683,* it states that William Bull lived at Sheldon Hall, Warwickshire, England. At the time of his death, his youngest son, William Bull, was rector of Sheldon Church in Warwickshire. Two other sons had come to South Carolina.

When the Sheldon Episcopal Church was built in South Carolina, an impressive life-size bronze statue of Prince William, son of George II, was placed over the portico of the building. The Bull coat of arms was built into a wall near the pew of Governor William Bull, and when Lieutenant Governor William Bull's remains were laid to rest, they were buried beneath the chancel of the church.

In the sanctuary stood a large font that was used in baptismal services. The font was supported by a pedestal decorated in the popular lion's claw motif. Many slaves, as well as their masters, were baptised at this font.

As the Revolution threatened, the statue of Prince William was removed and taken to Sheldon Hall, where the Bulls kept it safe. At this time the grounds of the church were being used for the practice of drill teams. Each time, the men of the militia carefully removed their firearms, which were secretly stored in the Bull family tomb. After drill the weapons went back to the burial ground.

The ruins of Old Sheldon Church.
Photograph by SID RHYNE.

After the burning of the church in 1779, Sheldon Church parishioners worshipped within the open walls. As fortunes came to the planters of indigo and rice, the parish grew, and in 1826 the restored building was consecrated. Soon afterward, church wardens received word that a Beaufort matron had a gift for Sheldon Episcopal Church. When they visited her, she handed them a heavy item wrapped in a rector's black silk robe. To their amazement, there gleaming before them was the communion silver of the parish. As the men looked over the chalices, an alms plate and other silver, the lady explained that the silver had been delivered to her by an English soldier during the war.

The second burning of Old Sheldon Church was just as devastating as the first, but again the walls didn't crumble. After that war, the planters' assets were gone, and although they tried to hold on during Reconstruction, the going was rough. But they never lost their respect for Sheldon Episcopal Church, and their descendants attend services on the grounds each year at noon on the second Sunday after Easter.

Today many artists come to sketch the stately vine-covered columns rising from the tangled growth at Sheldon Church. The burial ground is also a point of interest. One impressive marker is inscribed: "Within this tomb lie the remains of Mary Bull, wife of John Bull, who died September, 1771, aged 69 years." The adjacent tomb is especially ornate, decorated with huge claw feet. It is inscribed: "Under this lies the body of Mary Middleton, a pious Christian, an affectionate wife, a tender mother, a dutiful daughter, and a sincere friend. Wife of Thomas Middleton. Died February 2nd, 1760 in the 37th year of her age."

Entrance to Wormsloe. The country's longest avenue of oaks.
Photograph by SID RHYNE.

Wormsloe—Built By A Noble

Early in the 1700s, a son was born to an English carpenter and his wife. They baptized him Noble, and he would become the patriarch of one of the noblest of American families.

Noble Jones became a carpenter like his father and worked in Lambeth, England, on the south bank of the Thames, completely unaware that he would figure prominently in the history of Georgia. He fell in love with Sarah Hack and wrote a poem for her, endeavoring to win her hand in marriage.

This was not sent . . . . *In compliment,*
Let us share . . . . *In joy and care,*
In my breast . . . . *My Heart Doth Rest,*
The love is true . . . . *That I owe you,*
Despise not me . . . . *For I love thee,*
Of all the rest . . . . *I love the best.*
The love I owe . . . . *I fain would show.*
O, that I might . . . . *Have thee my wight.*
What I call mine . . . . *Shall be thine.*
I shorely Die . . . . *If you Deny,*
I do love none . . . . *But thee alone,*
I'll rather Die . . . . *Than not comply,*
Love is heard . . . . *Boath plain & clare*
As I affect thee . . . . *So respect me,*
No turtle dove . . . . *Hath firmer love,*
My love by this . . . . *Presented is.*
Heart and hand . . . . *At your command,*
The sight of thee . . . . *Is life to me,*
Inconstancy . . . . *I live and die,*
I am yours . . . . *While life endures.*

The poem must have worked, and Noble Jones and Sarah Hack were married at St. James Westminster on July 30, 1723. Their first child was a daughter, Mary.

Among the 114 colonists who came to Georgia with General James Edward Oglethorpe were Noble Jones, his wife, and two indentured servants. They arrived safely in Georgia, a colony supported by the Trustees, who resided in England. In 1736 Noble Jones requested a lease for the property on the Isle of Hope, ten miles south of Savannah. When he was granted the lease, he celebrated by naming the property Wormslow.

Almost as soon as he had obtained the property he began constructing a house of tabby. By this time, many buildings of tabby were in existence and they were found to be durable in the semi-tropical climate. Besides that, the ingredients of oyster shells, lime and sand were plentiful. (The practice of building structures of tabby had probably come from the Spanish, for as early as 1509 Ponce de Leon's house in Puerto Rico was built of *tapia*.) The Jones house contained five rooms, three of which had tabby floors. One room had a floor of wood, and two had flooring of square brick tiles. Spelling of the name was changed to Wormsloe.

When work on the house was completed, Jones turned his attention to cultivating a plantation that would produce rice, cotton, cattle, and silk. Although most of the Georgia coastal plantations had many acres of rice land, there was also land that was excellent for general farming purposes. The Trustees were particularly interested in the cultivation of silk, and they earnestly believed that a silk industry could rise up from the Georgia coastal plantations. The planters set out mulberry trees, the leaves of which provided food for silkworms, but the silk industry never got a toehold in Georgia.

A son was born to Noble and Sarah and they named him Noble Wimberly Jones. When the colony was royalized, the first Noble Jones was offered a seat on the coveted Governor's Council. Someone once said that in the beginning there is a time of service to your country, then a time of reward for your service. Noble Jones was now in the time of service to his country—England. But his son became a fierce Loyalist.

Finally, the conflict of father against son became a painful one. Noble Wimberly was glad that his father had not witnessed the fires and broken bodies that came as a result of the Revolution. His father had died prior to the Revolutionary War.

Savannah fell to the British in 1778 and Noble Wimberly escaped to Charleston, where he was arrested by the British when that city was captured. The next year he was paroled, and from that date until his death in 1805, he practiced medicine in Savannah. His son George also became a physician.

Dr. George Jones was the third master of Wormsloe and his son, Noble Wimberly Jones II, followed him at the plantation. Noble Wimberly Jones II married Sarah Fenwick Campbell and they had several children, one daughter being born only two years prior to her father's death. A son of this Noble Jones, George Noble Jones, had strong ties in Charleston and Newport, Rhode Island, and he had a taste for the good life. A colony of

Kingscote, a charming Gothic revival cottage built in 1838 by Richard Upjohn for George Noble Jones of Savannah, Georgia. The mansion stands on Bellevue Avenue in Newport, Rhode Island, and is open to the public.
Courtesy of The Preservation Society of Newport County.

planters from South Carolina and Georgia had built magnificent homes in Newport; there they spent their summers away from the humidity and diseases that were caused by mosquitoes breeding in the low-lying rice fields. Henry Middleton, of Middleton Place near Charleston, had bought an impressive house that had been constructed by Alexander MacGregor, a Scottish stone mason. While visiting there in the 1830s, George Jones fell in love with Delia Tudor Gardiner, a descendant of an original Rhode Island settler. After George married Delia, he toyed with the idea of building a home in Newport that would be their summer dwelling. The plans were interrupted in 1836 when Delia died.

By September 1839, George Jones was actively planning the construction of his home in Newport and he wrote to Richard Upjohn, a Welshman and designer of Trinity Church, on lower Broadway in New York City: *"Having recently purchased a lot of land in this place* [Newport] *I propose, for the future to make it my summer residence."*

The first set of plans submitted to George were not to his liking and a second set were drawn up. The building was designed with such compelling attractions that it was felt the occupants would need to venture no further than the cozy confines, unless to dine out. During construction, George returned to Georgia and married Mary Wallace Savage Nuttall, the widow of a wealthy Virginian. Mary had her own riches, including plantations and slaves.

When the mansion was completed, it was even more alluring than expected. The gables were trimmed with carved pinnacles and serpentine bargeboards, and the eaves were bordered with pendant trefoils. A long porch on the east side was constructed of lattice. George Jones' new home was not a hideaway; rather, it attracted its fair share of the country's oldest, wealthiest and most influential families. Mary Jones became the perfect hostess at the Newport mansion that was referred to as "the cottage." The cellars were stocked with fine wines, and after-dinner entertainment consisted of playing charades. Newporters preferred privacy and quiet elegance; they returned year after year as faithfully as the tides, to savor the summers on this most spectacular coast.

A fence designed by Upjohn surrounded the grounds at the Jones mansion. The gardens were laid out when the house was under construction. Beyond the fence, to the west, lay Newport harbor. Open country, dotted with farms, was the scene of the southern exposure, and across the road called Bellevue lay a large marsh area that was filled with wildlife.

Just prior to the Civil War, the funiture, many volumes of books, the inventory of the wine cellar, and a gold-trimmed French porcelain dinner service for twenty-four were shipped to Savannah on the last boat to arrive there before the blockade. The furniture and five barrels of porcelain lay in a warehouse.

When the Civil War broke out, Mrs. Jones and the children were in Paris; George Jones was in Savannah. The title of their Newport home was transferred, and in 1863 the house was sold to William Henry King. Finally, the furniture and porcelain were taken from the warehouse and distributed among the heirs of George Jones, in Savannah.

Today one can view Kingscote, the Newport mansion, and visit the magnificent avenue of oaks in Savannah. Visitors frequently stroll over to the tabby ruins that mark the location of Noble Jones' fortified house, begun about 1739. The visitor center contains an excellent 16-minute slide presentation and pictorial history on the colonization of Savannah. The Noble Jones family, owners of Wormsloe Plantation for over two centuries, are featured.

Wormsloe is famous for its avenue of oaks—the longest in America, at one and a half miles long and containing 400 oak trees. Wormsloe has been the home of the Jones family since 1745. Near the avenue of oaks there stands a gracious home inhabited by the remaining family members. They have a huge black dog named Noble.

Although the family has retained sixty-five and a half acres, the Georgia Department of Natural Resources operates the remaining 822 acres. Wormsloe is a twenty-minute drive from downtown Savannah, and it is a "must see" for visitors. The historic site is located at 7501 Skidaway Road, eight miles southeast of Savannah. If traveling on I-95, take Exit 16 and proceed twelve miles toward Savannah on GA 205. Turn right onto Montgomery Crossroads and drive 3.2 miles until the road dead ends. Turn right onto Skidaway Road and proceed eight-tenths of a mile to the impressive entrance.

Epilogue

The wealthy northerners who bought southern plantations for use as private hunting preserves—as well as for the status of owning a little piece of a historic colony—were soon to discover that their station in life in the new surroundings was apocryphal. Not only were they not dubbed the toast of Charleston, alongside the Rhetts and Pinckneys and Middletons, they were considered gauche outsiders.

Charleston had a way of ruling out, rather than accepting. The professions ruled out the trades; the inland cotton planters ruled out the professions; the sea island cotton planters ruled out the inland planters; and the rice planters ruled out the sea island cotton planters. The planters were the bluebloods, "the quality," the aristocracy; and their descendants intended to keep it that way. If, as we hope, there will always be a *South*, there will most certainly always be a blueblood. But the question persists: what exactly constitutes a "person of quality"?

The southern gentleman's superior position in society was determined not by law, nor by popular vote, nor, strictly speaking, by class. He was in a class by himself! He had scripted the first, unwritten law: only a southern gentleman could be a southern gentleman.

From the battlefield at Yorktown, where aristocrats and commoners fought side by side, to the Jockey Club's Washington Race Course, where the planters showed off their thoroughbreds, the Charlestonian proved himself one of the world's wonders: a southern gentleman. It wasn't a question of snobbery, of which the gentlemen were constantly accused; it was simply that people born outside the planter gentry did not count.

The unspoken laws governing aristocracy excluded the northern *invaders*. The fact that the Hutton brothers owned Prospect Hill, Laurel Spring, and other plantations and Bernard Baruch owned a barony didn't make them gentlemen. They were merely entrepreneurs. The heirs of planters endured; entrepreneurs were in and out of vogue. The aristocrats were never *in* vogue. They were above it!

The rest of the world, to them, was a mere incident. Not even the Pearly Gates opened to a region more desirable than the world of the Charleston bluebloods.

Although the southern gentlemen had adopted that unapproachable style from the English, they felt they owned the patent, and they didn't want the patent questioned by a person not considered "of the quality." In some cities, Paris as an example, there is a high society that seldom admits outsiders into its midst. The politicians there live in their own circle; the bourgeoisie congregate with one another. Descendants of southern planters hobnobbed with each other to the same marked degree. On Charleston's Tradd Street, the aristocracy lived next door to descendants of slaves, and since they were more or less in the same great planter circle, they accepted one another's presence with worthiness, even if you didn't see them at the same table.

It was fitting that the dialect, like the atmosphere, was just a little different. "Charleston brogue" was the speech of choice of the bluebloods. Just as the aristocracy took a little more time to live and to think, so they talked. "Garden" often became "gyarden." "Car" became "cyar."

A southern gentleman's values were those of his father and his grandfather and his great-grandfather. He was true to his standards. The subject of money was most distasteful. A gentleman simply never mentioned it. So, to find themselves at the turn of the twentieth century at the mercy of the gentlemen of means who resided on the old plantations was a real discomfort. The plantations of that period were as different from the originals as the present owners were from the former.

Newspapers once published J. Motte Alston's description of his grandfather's plantation. According to Alston, family house servants wore dark green broadcloth coats and vests trimmed in silver braid with red facings. Their trousers were of green plush. The Alston coach, sporting the family's colors of dark green and red was adorned with the family coat of arms, which featured the motto "Immotus." Daily life on the old plantations was colorful and glorious. The lifestyle of the wealthy northerners was simply a common hallelujah in comparison.

Dispatches from the social world of the northerners frequently made the Charleston newspapers:

> Mr. and Mrs. Nelson Doubleday are guests at Mr. Charles L. Lawrance's White Hall Plantation. Mr. and Mrs. Donald Dodge are at their plantation on Edisto Island. Mr. and Mrs.

> A. H. Caspary are at Bonny Doone. They have as their guests Mr. and Mrs. John R. Wellington of New York. Mr. and Mrs. William R. Coe are at their plantation, Cherokee, near Yemassee. Mr. Eugene duPont of Wilmington, Delaware, is at his plantation home, Combahee. Mr. Nicholas G. Roosevelt is at his plantation, Gippy, in Berkeley County.

All in all, as a southern gentleman was quoted saying, "The Huttons were not accepted here. They were noveau riche. My first mother-in-law, Mrs. Gaud, whose relatives were Middletons, said the Huttons were never one of us. The Middletons started Newport. Finally, they left, as they wrote in a letter, 'Newport has gone to the dogs. People like the Vanderbilts and Astors are coming here now.' But the Huntingtons and duPonts were accepted. They were believed to be aristocracy. They were one of us."

Perhaps, when all is said and done, the Huntingtons and the duPonts fit in because they never *tried* to be "one of us."

Bibliography

Allston, Susan Lowndes. *Brookgreen Waccamaw in the Carolina Low Country*. Charleston, SC: Nelson's Southern Printing & Publishing Co., 1956.

Baruch, Bernard M. *Baruch: My Own Story*. New York: Henry Holt and Co., 1957.

Bull, Henry DeSaussure. *All Saints' Church, Waccamaw: The Parish, The Place, The People, 1739–1768*. Georgetown, SC: Winyah Press, 1968.

Childs, Arney R., ed. *Rice Planter and Sportsman: The Recollections of J. Motte Alston, 1821–1909*. Columbia, SC: University of South Carolina Press, 1953.

Coit, Margaret L. *Mr. Baruch*. New York: Houghton Mifflin Co., 1957.

Devereux, Anthony Q. *The Rice Princes: A Rice Epoch Revisited*. Columbia, SC: State Printing Co., 1973.

Esterby, J. H., ed. *The South Carolina Rice Plantation*. Chicago: University of Chicago, 1945.

Glennie, Alexander. *Sermons Preached on Plantations in Congregations of Slaves*. Charleston, SC: A. E. Miller, 1844.

Graydon, Nell S. *Eliza of Wappoo*. Columbia, SC : R. L. Bryan Co., 1967.

Hooker, Richard J., ed. *A Colonial Plantation Cookbook: The Receipt Book of Harriott Pinckney Horry 1770*. Columbia, SC: University of South Carolina Press, 1984.

Joyner, Charles. *Down by the Riverside: A South Carolina Slave Community*. Chicago: University of Illinois, 1984.

Lachicotte, Alberta Morel. *Georgetown Rice Plantations*. Columbia, SC: State Printing Co., 1955.

Linder, Suzanne C. *Atlas of Rice Plantations of the ACE Basin*. Columbia, SC: South Carolina Department of Archives and History, 1996.

Ludlum, David M. *Early American Hurricanes 1491–1870*. Boston: American Meteorological Society, 1963.

Prevost, Charlotte Kaminski, and Effie Leland Wilder. *Pawley's Island—A Living Legend*. Columbia, SC: State Printing Co., 1972.

Pringle, Elizabeth Allston. *Chronicles of Chicora Wood*. Atlanta: Cherokee Publishing Co., 1976.

——— (Patience Pennington). *A Woman Rice Planter*. New York: Macmillan Co., 1928.

Quattlebaum, Paul. *The Land Called Chicora*. Gainesville: University of Florida Press, 1956.

Ravenel, Mrs. St. Julien. *Charleston: The Place and the People*. New York: Macmillan Co., 1912.

Rogers, George C., Jr. *The History of Georgetown County, South Carolina*. Columbia, SC: University of South Carolina Press, 1970.

Rutledge, Archibald. *Home by the River*. Indianapolis: Bobbs-Merrill Co., 1941.

Rutledge, Irvine H. *We Called Him Flintlock*. Columbia, SC: R. L. Bryan Co., 1974.

Savage, Henry, Jr. *River of the Carolinas: The Santee*. Chapel Hill: University of North Carolina Press, 1956.

Willcox, Clarke A. *Musings of a Hermit*. Charleston, SC: Walker, Evans & Cogswell Co., 1968.

Williams, Frances Leigh. *Plantation Patriot: A Biography of Eliza Lucas Pinckney*. New York: Harcourt, Brace & World, Inc., 1967.

NEWSPAPERS

Charleston News and Courier, Various clippings on file at Charleston County Library.

New York Times, December 20, 1955 and April 26, 1964.

The Georgetown Times, A Bicentennial Supplement.

San Francisco Examiner, August 14, 1900.

Bridgeport Sunday Post, August 10, 1958.

Atlanta Constitution, October 14, 1983.

MAGAZINES

The Sunday Republican Magazine (Waterbury, Connecticut), January 29, 1967.

Yankee, August 1970.